JAMIE'S STORY

It was the story I might have told Susan last night had Jamie's phone call not shattered the moment. As he spoke now, I became all of us. I was Jamie himself, confessing not to a brutal knife murder, no, but to murder nonetheless—the inexorable suffocation of his second marriage. I was Susan listening to the confession I did not make last night, but which Jamie now made *for* me. *Finally, I was the victim Maureen, unable to escape the blade that came at me relentlessly in this fatal blood-spattered cage.*

GOLDILOCKS
by
ED McBAIN

GOLDILOCKS

Ed Mcbain

This low-priced Golden Apple Book has been completely reset in a type face designed for easy reading, and was printed from new plates. It contains the complete text of the original hard-cover edition.
NOT ONE WORD HAS BEEN OMITTED.

GOLDILOCKS
A Golden Apple Publication / published by arrangement with Arbor House Publishing Company, Inc.

Golden Apple edition / December 1984

Golden Apple is a trademark of Golden Apple Publications

For information address: Golden Apple Publishers, 666 Fifth Avenue, New York, N.Y. 10103.

ISBN 0-553-19791-6

PRINTED IN CANADA

COVER PRINTED IN U.S.A.

0 9 8 7 6 5 4 3 2 1

This is for the Tuesday night players:

BERNIE BURROUGHS
AL FIELDS
SONNY FOX
RON KING
DAN KONOVER
STANLEY MACHENBERG
SIDNEY MILWE
JOE WAXBERG
HARVEY WEISS

1

THERE WAS a white patrol car parked at the curb outside the house. It's dome lights and headlights were out. The street at one A.M. was silent, the neighbors alseep. I pulled in behind the car, cut the engine, and started walking to where Jamie stood in the moonlight, talking to a uniformed policeman. The jacaranda tree behind him was leafless, blossomless. Out on the bayou behind the house, I could hear the chugging of the fishing boat I'd seen while crossing the bridge from Lucy's Circle. There were only saltwater mullet in the shallow waters on this side of the bridge, and they would not strike a hook; the commercial fishermen were spreading their nets, circling, circling.

Jamie looked drawn and pale. He was forty-six years old—ten years older than I—but in the pale moonlight he seemed much younger, or perhaps only more vulnerable. He was wearing a faded blue T-shirt, white trousers, and blue sneakers. The patrolman was visibly perspiring. Sweat stained the armholes of his blue shirt, stood out in beads on his forehead. I did not know whether he had yet been inside the house. He watched me as I approached.

"I'm Matthew Hope," I said. "Dr. Purchase's attorney." I don't know why I immediately addressed myself to the patrolman, rather than to Jamie. I guess I was trying to protect Jamie from the very beginning, letting it be known to the Law that I myself was a lawyer who expected no hanky-panky with a client's rights.

"He call you then?" the patrolman asked.

"Yes, he did."

"When was that, sir?"

"At about a quarter to one. Ten minutes ago."

"I didn't get the radio dispatch till five minutes ago," the patrolman said. He made it sound like an accusation.

"That's right," I said, "he called me first. I advised him to notify the police."

"Would it be all right if I went inside the house now?" the patrolman asked.

"Yes," Jamie said dully.

"You don't have to come with me, you don't want to."

"I would . . . rather not," Jamie said.

"That's all right, sir," the patrolman said, and touched Jamie's shoulder briefly and surprisingly. He flashed his torch over the lawn then, and walked swiftly to the front door, weaving his way through the sprinkler heads like a brokenfield runner. The circle of light illuminated the brass doorknob. He twisted it tentatively, as if expecting the door to be locked, and then he opened the door and went inside.

Alone with Jamie, I said, "I'm going to ask you again what I asked you on the phone . . ."

"I didn't do it," he said at once.

"Tell me the truth, Jamie?"

"That's the truth."

"Because if you *did*, I want to know right this minute."

"I didn't."

"All right, do you have any idea who *might* have done it?"

"No, Matt, I don't."

"Why'd you call me instead of the police?"

"I don't know why. I guess . . . you're my lawyer, Matt, I guess I thought . . . something like this. I don't know."

Another patrol car was pulling in toward the curb. No siren, no dome lights. The man inside cut the engine and got out. Hitching up his trousers, he walked to where

Jamie and I were standing near the naked jacaranda. He was a huge man. I'm six feet two inches tall and weigh a hundred and ninety pounds, but I felt dwarfed beside him. There were sergeant's stripes on the sleeve of his blue uniform. He was perspiring even more profusely than the patrolman—the temperature that day had hit ninety-nine degrees, and it was now eighty-six and oppressively humid. This was weather more suited to August than the last day of February.

"Sergeant Hascomb," he said, and politely touched the peak of his hat. "I'm looking for whoever called the police."

"I did," Jamie said.

"Could you tell me your name, sir?"

"James Purchase."

"I ran over the minute I caught it on the radio," Hascomb said. "I knew Furley'd be calling me, anyway—this is a signal five. I'm his supervisor." I had the impression his size made him feel awkward with men smaller than himself. He took a handkerchief from his back pocket, removed the hat from his head, and wiped his brow. "Is he inside now, is that it?"

"Yes," I said.

"I'm sorry, sir, you're . . . ?"

"Matthew Hope. I'm Dr. Purchase's attorney."

"I see," he said. "Well, excuse me," he said, and walked toward the front door. Before he went into the house, he wiped the sweatband of the hat with his handkerchief. He came out again a few moments later and walked swiftly past us to the car. Black batwing blots of perspiration covered the back of his shirt. I saw him reaching for the car radio. His face was ashen.

I am not a criminal lawyer.

I'd practiced law for seven years in Illinois before moving to Calusa, and I'd been practicing law here in the state of Florida for the past three years, but I'd never represented anyone involved in a crime. The first thing I'd asked Jamie on the telephone was whether or not he wanted me to contact a criminal lawyer. Wait, that's not quite true. I first asked him if he'd committed the murders. When he assured me he hadn't, I then reminded him that I was not a criminal lawyer and asked if he wanted me to call a good one. Jamie replied, "If I didn't kill them, why do I need a criminal lawyer?" I had no answer for him at the time. I'd simply advised him to call the police at once, and told him I'd be there as soon as I was dressed. Now, at one-thirty in the morning, with law enforcement officers and related personnel swarming all over the house and the grounds, I felt completely out of my element and wished I had insisted on expert help.

There were three marked patrol cars at the curb, and the patrolmen from those cars had set up barricades at either end of Jacaranda Drive. Inside the barricades, there were four vehicles belonging to the captain in command of the Detective Bureau, the two plainclothes detectives he'd assigned to the case, and the assistant medical examiner. The man from the State's Attorney's office had parked his car across the street, behind the Ford Econoline van from the Criminalistics Unit. The ambulance from Southern Medical was backed into the driveway, its rear doors open. The activity had wakened neighbors all up and down the street. They stood just outside the barricades, whispering, speculating, stopping one or another of the patrolmen to ask what had happened. Most of the neighbors were still in pajamas and robes. The moonlight illuminated the lawn and the street and the house.

"Who's in charge here?" the medical examiner asked.

"I am."

The detective's name was George Ehrenberg. He looked to be about my age, maybe a year or so younger, thirty-four or -five. He had red hair that fell onto his forehead like a rust stain. His beetling brows were red, too, and his eyes were a brown so dark as to be almost black. There were freckles on the bridge of his nose and his cheeks. He was wearing a loud plaid summer-weight jacket and dark blue trousers, blue socks and brown loafers. Under the jacket, a wine-colored polo shirt was open at the throat. He was a big man, like most of the other policemen who were now at the house.

"I'm finished in there, you can have them now," the m.e. said. He was referring to the corpses of Jamie's wife and children. "Your cause of death is multiple stab wounds," he said. "Hard to say which of them was the fatal cut. Whoever done it . . ."

"This here's the husband here," Ehrenberg said.

"Sorry," the m.e. said. "Anyway, the coroner'll pinpoint it for you. Sorry," he said again, and walked to where a blue Chevrolet was parked at the curb.

Ehrenberg went over to where his partner was standing with the technician from Criminalistics. I hadn't caught the partner's name. He was a small dark man with intensely blue eyes. Ehrenberg said a few words to him, and he nodded and then went into the house with the technician. Ehrenberg came back to Jamie and me.

"Would it be all right to ask Dr. Purchase some questions?" he said.

"He's not a suspect here, is he?"

"No, sir, he's not. I can read him his rights if you want me to, sir, but this is just a normal field investigation, and I'm really not required to. If you want me to, though, I'd be happy . . ."

"No, no, that's all right," I said.

"Well then, *is* it all right, sir? To ask him some questions?"

"Yes, go ahead," I said.

"Dr. Purchase, I'm assuming you didn't kill your own wife and kids, am I right in assuming that?"

His voice was only mildly southern, with scarcely a trace of dialect. You had to listen very closely to catch the occasional softened vowel or missing final consonant. His manner was friendly and pleasant, even though he was here to ask about bloody murder.

"I didn't kill them," Jamie said.

"Good, and I'm further assuming you want to help us find whoever *did* kill them, am I right in assuming that, Dr. Purchase?"

"Yes."

"Can you think of anyone who might have done a thing like this?"

"No," Jamie said.

"Have you had any threatening letters or phone calls recently?"

"No, I haven't."

"You're a physician, is that right, sir?"

"Yes."

"Do you practice here in Calusa?"

"Yes, I have an office in Belvedere Medical."

"Would any of your patients have had reason to be angry at you, or to . . ."

"No, none that I can think of."

"How about your nurses? Any arguments with them recently?"

"No."

"Do you pay them good salaries?"

"I do."

"Any of them ask for a raise recently?"

"I gave them both raises only last month."

"What about your associates?"

"I'm in practice alone, I have no associates."

"Do you have any professional rivals who might want to harm you or your family?"

"None that I can think of."

"How about any recent disputes with the families of patients you've treated? Anything like that?"

"No."

"Have you been dunning anyone for nonpayment of bills?"

"No."

"Dr. Purchase, I'm going to ask you something personal now, but I need to know the answer because it's important. Were either you or your wife fooling around outside the marriage?"

"We were very happily married."

"How long have you been married, Dr. Purchase?"

"Eight years."

"This your first marriage?"

"No."

"Is your first wife still alive?"

"Yes."

"She live here in Calusa?"

"Yes."

"Any children by the first marriage?"

"Two."

"Where do they live?"

"My daughter's been living in New York for the past three years. My son's here in Calusa."

"How old are they?"

"My daughter's twenty-two. My son is twenty."

"Had any family arguments with them lately?"

"No."

"You get along fine with them, is that it?"

"I get along. . . ." Jamie shrugged. "Well enough," he said. "They didn't much like the idea of my divorcing their mother, but that was eight years ago, and I'm sure they're over it now."

"When's the last time you saw your daughter?"

"At Christmas."

"Here in Calusa?"

"No, in New York. I went up there to see her, we exchanged gifts. It was very pleasant."

"And your son?"

"He was here for dinner last Tuesday night."

"He get along with your second wife?"

"Yes, they got along fine."

"What's his name, sir?"

"Michael."

"And he lives where?"

"On a boat. It's docked at Pirate's Cove."

"Out on Stone Crab Key?"

"Yes."

"Does he live alone?"

"There's a girl he lives with."

"What's her name?"

"I don't know. I've never met her."

"How about your daughter? What's her name?"

"Karin."

"And your former wife?"

"Betty."

"I'll need their addresses later."

"Fine."

"Dr. Purchase, from what I understand, you weren't home much of the night tonight. Is that correct?"

"That's right, I was out playing poker."

"What time did you leave the house, sir?"

"At twenty to eight."

"Where did you play?"

"On Whisper Key."

"Somebody's house?"

"Yes. A man named Art Kramer. On Henchey Pass Road."

"What time did you get there?"

"A few minutes before eight. The traffic was very light."

"Went over the Santa Maria Bridge, did you?"

"Yes."

"How many players in the game?"

"Seven."

"I'll need their names. I'd appreciate it if you wrote them down for me later, Dr. Purchase. Their names and addresses."

"I don't know all the names. There were some new players."

"Whichever ones you remember."

"All right."

"What time did you leave the game, Dr. Purchase?"

"A little before eleven."

"How come?"

"I was losing heavily."

"You came straight home, did you?"

"No."

"Where *did* you go?"

"I stopped for a drink at The Innside Out."

"How long were you there?"

"I left there at about twelve-thirty. A little before twelve-thirty, I guess it was."

"How many drinks did you have?"

"Two."

"You got there at what time?"

"At about eleven."

"And you left at twelve-thirty."

"A little before twelve-thirty. About twenty after."

"See anyone you know there?"

"No."

"No one who might recognize you, huh?"

"No. Unless . . . I don't know. I was sitting at the bar, maybe the bartender would remember me. I really couldn't say."

"But you don't know the bartender personally, do you?"

"No, I don't."

"What time did you get back to the house, Dr. Purchase?"

"About twenty to one, I guess it was."

"See anything unusual when you drove up?"

"Nothing."

"Anybody outside?"

"No."

"Were the lights on?"

"Yes."

"Was that usual?"

"Maureen always left them on when I wasn't home."

"How'd you enter the house, Dr. Purchase? The front door?"

"No, I put the car in the garage and then went around to the side door. The kitchen door."

"Was the door locked?"

"Yes, it was."

"You used your key to open it?"

"Yes."

"Do you play poker every Sunday night?"

"Every other Sunday night."

"That's a fixed routine, is it?"

"Yes, more or less. We sometimes have to cancel a game because we can't get enough players that particular week."

"Is it the same players each week?"

"We try to keep the same players, yes. We have a list of standbys if one of them can't—"

"I'd like the names of the players now, if you don't mind," Ehrenberg said.

An intern and an ambulance attendant were carrying out Maureen's body when Ehrenberg placed his call. A rubber sheet covered her. Her left hand dangled over the side of the stretcher. There were cuts on the fingers and palm. The ring finger was almost severed, hacked to the bone. A pair of patrolmen carried out the second stretcher. Jamie's little girls were six and four years old respectively. The last time I'd seen them alive was two Saturdays ago, when I'd taken my own family to swim in Jamie's pool. Emily, the six-year-old, had told me then that her boyfriend had braces on his teeth. She asked me if I thought braces were bad. I told her braces were fine. She seemed dubious.

Ehrenberg had tented a handkerchief over his hand before picking up the receiver, and he'd dialed the number with the eraser end of a pencil. I thought this excessively theatrical, but I guessed he knew what he was doing. Into the phone, he said, "Mr. Kramer? This is Detective Ehrenberg of the Calusa Police Department, I'm sorry to be calling you this time of night."

Two more patrolmen were carrying out the third stretcher. The intern and the ambulance attendant were on their way back to the bedroom. They stopped short when they saw the stretcher coming out. The intern looked annoyed. He shook his head and went out the front door again. The ambulance attendant said, "You need any help?" and the patrolman at the front end of the stretcher said, "No, we've got it," and all three of them went out of the house.

On the phone, Ehrenberg said, "I wanted to ask you, sir, whether a Dr. James Purchase was at your home this evening. Uh-huh. What time did he get there, sir? Uh-huh. And what time did he leave? Uh-huh. Well, thank you very much, sir, I certainly am obliged. Thank you, sir," he said again, and put the receiver back on the cradle, and his handkerchief back in his pocket. "Well, that's fine," he said to Jamie. "You've got to forgive me checking up like this, Dr. Purchase, but we've got to touch all the bases with a homicide. You didn't plan on sleeping the night here, did you?"

"I hadn't given it any thought," Jamie said.

" 'Cause there'll be men here till morning at least, there's lots to do. You'd be better off at a friend's house or a motel, you don't mind my suggesting it."

"Thank you," Jamie said. "I'll pack some things."

He started toward the master bedroom, and then stopped. He shook his head then, and turned abruptly, and walked out of the house. I went after him. It was ten minutes past two when we left the scene of the crime.

2

I OFFERED Jamie our guest room, but he said he wanted to be alone, said he needed some time alone to pull himself together. He had not cried yet. I kept expecting tears, but none came. At the stoplight on the other end of the causeway, he told me he desperately needed a drink. So instead of making a left turn toward the airport and the string of small motels lining either side of the highway north, I turned right, hoping to find an open bar among those scattered along the South Trail. I was frankly dubious—but Jamie's hands were beginning to tremble in his lap.

The eastern rim of Calusa Bay is jaggedly defined by U.S. 41, more familiarly known as the Tamiami Trail. It's my partner Frank's belief that "Tamiami" is redneck for "To Miami." He may be right. If you follow 41 south, it eventually leads to Alligator Alley, which then crosses the Florida peninsula to the east coast. I was driving south now, looking for an open bar, wondering if there might be one out on Whisper Key. There are five keys off Calusa's mainland, but only three of them—Stone Crab, Sabal and Whisper—run north-south, paralleling the opposite shore. Flamingo Key and Lucy's Key are situated like stepping-stones across the water, connecting the mainland to Sabal and Stone Crab. Beyond the keys is the Gulf of Mexico. Sail out due west from Calusa, and eventually you'll make landfall in Corpus Christi, Texas.

I found an open cocktail lounge just below the Cross River Shopping Center. The neon signs outside were still on, and there were several cars angle-parked against the stucco front wall of the building. But the moment we stepped inside, a waitress in a short black skirt and a low-cut white blouse said, "Sorry, we're closed." She seemed altogether too young and too fresh to be serving whiskey in the empty hours of the night. The bartender was pouring a fresh drink for one of the four men seated at the bar. The waitress caught my glance and said, "They've been here for a while, you see. Really, we're just closing." At the other end of the room, two young men were putting chairs up on tables and a third was beginning to mop the floor.

"Well, why don't you just serve us till it's time to lock up, okay?" I said, and smiled.

The waitress' name was Sandy. It said so in white letters on a little black plastic rectangle pinned to her blouse. She said, "Well . . ." and looked at the bartender. The bartender shrugged philosophically, and then nodded us over to the bar. We took stools closest to the door, away from the drone of the television set. A late-night movie was showing. Something with Humphrey Bogart. I wondered if the waitress knew who Humphrey Bogart was.

"What'll you have?" the bartender asked.

"Jamie?"

"Bourbon on the rocks."

"I'll have a Dewar's and soda."

The bartender nodded. On the television screen, Bogart was telling an actress I didn't recognize that she was good, she was very good. Jamie kept staring at his hands on the bar-top, almost as if willing them to stop shaking. The bartender brought the drinks and Jamie lifted his glass at once and swallowed half the bourbon in it. He put the glass down on the bar-top, and then the tears came. I put my arm around him.

"Oh, Jesus, Matt," he said, "I never . . . I never saw . . . oh, Jesus."

"Take it easy," I said.

"So much . . . *blood*, Oh, Jesus. All over the walls, she must've grabbed for the walls . . . like a damn cage . . . like trying to get out of a damn cage. Trapped in there with . . ."

"All right," I said. "All right, Jamie, come on now."

The drinkers lined up along the bar seemed lulled into a stupor by the television screen, but the bartender had turned to look at Jamie. I kept patting his shoulder comfortingly, and he kept sobbing and trying to choke back the sobs, and finally he took out his handkerchief and dried his eyes and blew his nose. He picked up the bourbon glass, drained it, and signaled to the bartender for a refill. As the bartender poured the fresh drink, he kept watching Jamie curiously. Even when he went back to the other end of the bar, he turned his head for a periodic look at him.

"The thing that froze me in the door the doorway was the *fury* of it," Jamie said. "The way who whoever did it had had just ripped and slashed . . . Jesus, Matt, I went in there, I . . . Jesus . . . "

"Okay," I said.

"So much blood," he said, and began sobbing again.

"Okay, Jamie."

"She . . . you know . . . she was my second-chance girl. I mean, how many chances do you get? Figure it out, how much time have I got left? I'm forty-six, what have I got left, another thirty years? It never works out the way you think it will, does it? Change your whole life, start a new family, never the way you think. This was my second chance."

I'd known Jamie for three years. I knew, of course, that Maureen was his second wife. I knew, too, that she was a registered nurse and that she'd worked for him in his Calusa office. I'd reviewed and revised his pension plan only recently and had seen in old records the name Maureen O'Donnell listed as an employee. Moreover, shortly after their marriage, the plan had paid out an accumulated six thousand dollars in benefits to Maureen O'Donnell Purchase upon the termination of her employment. I deduced that theirs had been an office romance, and that it had led to Jamie's divorce and subsequent remarriage. But I had never known the details of their relationship, and had never asked for them; locker room confidences are a form of male bonding I normally do not encourage.

It embarrassed me now to hear Jamie talk about personal matters he would otherwise have kept to himself. The bartender was facing the television screen, but there was something about the erectness of his head that told me he was alert to every word Jamie uttered. Across the room, one of the young men stacking the chairs said something in Spanish, and the one mopping the floor began laughing. The laughter was soft, it echoed guitars and fans and black lace shawls. The waitress looked at her watch. There was no one left at the tables to serve, I wondered why she simply didn't go home. It occurred to me that she was waiting for the bartender.

"Fell in love with her the minute I saw her," Jamie said, and blew his nose again. "I knew this was my second chance. Matt, the first marriage had been dead from day one. Maureen walked into that office, she'd been sent by the registry, the nurse I'd had before her was pregnant and had to leave the job. She walked in there, Jesus, I'd never seen anything so beautiful in my life. I knew this was it, I knew I had to have her. I'd been playing around with other women for almost six years by then, but this was something else, this was . . . I don't know. I'd never believed in anything like this, but it was happening, she was there, she was suddenly in my life."

I signaled to the bartender for another drink. I didn't need another drink, I didn't even want another drink, but I was hopeful that a break in the conversation would turn Jamie in another direction. I truly did not want to hear about his affair with Maureen. When I was still living in Chicago, I used to see men walking along Michigan Boulevard, talking to themselves. Big cities do that to people. Once you're reduced to anonymity, it doesn't matter if you go around holding a spirited conversation with no one but yourself. Anybody noticing you will shake his head and say, "Crazy," but he won't know *who's* crazy. Just some faceless lunatic ambling along in private solitary discourse, arms waving. Jamie was like that now. Ostensibly, he was talking to me; on the surface, this was a dialogue. But it was more like a monologue that flowed from somewhere in his unconscious, as if the brutal fact of murder had rendered him anonymous, the weight of the tragedy granting him both license and sanctuary.

I felt like an eavesdropper.

"My first wife was frigid, I told you that, didn't I?" he said. The bartender was standing not a foot away from him, pouring Scotch into my glass, openly interested in Jamie's words. Jamie seemed not to notice him. I looked up into the bartender's face, directly into his eyes. He turned away and walked back toward where Bogart was talking to the brunette with bobbed hair.

"She was in analysis for four years, wait, five years I think it was. Yes. Woman in Tampa. Yes. You begin to think it's *your* fault, do you know what I mean? Begin to think there's something wrong with what you're doing, she lays there like, you know, like a . . ." His voice trailed, I had the impression he'd been about to say "corpse." He nodded, sipped at his drink, put the glass down again. "She came home one night, must've been six o'clock, a little after. I forget what time her hour was, three-thirty, four, something like that. She came in all smiles, six o'clock. Took my hand, led me into the bedroom. This was ten years ago, she was a few years late with her precious orgasm. I'd been through half her close friends by then, and was already involved with Maureen. Few years too late, my darling wife with her glorious orgasm. Too late."

Just last month, I'd had a telephone conversation with his former wife. They still owned as joint tenants a piece of land in Sarasota, and they'd had an offer for it that was ten thousand higher than the minimum specified in their separation agreement. Betty Purchase had agreed to the deal and then abruptly backed out of it when Jamie missed sending his usual monthly alimony check. I did not know at the time that Jamie had no intention of ever paying her another cent. He mentioned that to me only after I'd had my conversation with her. On the phone, I told her if she didn't go ahead with the sale, the real estate agent was well within his rights to sue her for his commission. She said, "Fuck you *and* the real estate agent." I warned her that my client was intent on making the sale, and that if she would not agree to it as earlier promised, I would sue for a partition sale. She said, "Go ahead and sue, Charlie," and then hung up.

"I met her at U.C.L.A.," Jamie said. "I was going to medical school there, she was an undergraduate. You know my son Michael . . ."

"Yes, I do."

"He's got the same coloring as his mother, black hair, brown eyes. Karin's different, she's got my blond hair, but Michael's the image of his mother, you couldn't possibly mistake him for anyone else's son. Tore him apart, the divorce did. He told me one night, he was crying in my arms, he said I'd lied to him all his life. Said that whenever his mother and I used to argue and he asked if we were getting a divorce—he used to ask that even when he was six years old—we'd always tell him 'No, no, people argue, that doesn't mean divorce, that's a healthy sign, Mike. People who don't fight are people who don't really care about each other.' I used to believe that, Matt, but it's bullshit, it really is. People who fight all the time are people having trouble."

He sighed, drained his glass, and signaled to the bartender for a refill. The bartender was starting down the bar, collecting his tabs. The chairs were stacked, the floor was mopped, the Bogart movie had ended. The waitress in the short black skirt was tapping her foot impatiently.

"Took us eighteen months to reach a settlement," Jamie said, "eighteen *months*, can you believe it? She got two hundred thousand in cash, plus the house we were living in, and thirty thousand a year in alimony. I'm a doctor, Matt, I'm not a millionaire, what she got represented everything I'd ever worked for. She sent Michael away to military school right after the divorce. Twelve years old, she sent him away. A school in Virginia. He wasn't even there for my wedding, I couldn't get him out of that damn school for the weekend. Betty sent him away on purpose, you can bet on that, to make sure I wouldn't see him too often. Her whole idea was to alienate the kids, make them hate their father for the terrible thing he'd done. She succeeded with both of them.

"I once heard Karin and Michael talking together—this was Christmastime, Michael was home from that goddamn concentration camp and the kids were spending the afternoon with us. Betty had dropped them off after they'd already celebrated the holiday at her house, this was maybe three or four in the afternoon. That was her pattern. Keep the kids for herself, keep them thinking forever and always that I'd committed a heinous crime. Maureen and I were living in a small house on Stone Crab, she was already pregnant with Emily by then, this was seven years ago.

"There was a deck on the house, overhanging the beach, and when it was high tide the ocean would come right in under the pilings and the house would shake. We never could keep the sheets dry in that house, everything was always damp. The kids were out on the deck, looking at the ocean, their backs to me, I guess they didn't hear me slide open the glass door. I heard Michael say, 'Did you see the necklace he gave Goldilocks?' and I realized he was referring to Maureen. That was what Betty called her. Goldilocks. And of course, the kids picked it up. There was such bitterness in Michael's voice . . ."

The bartender was standing in front of him; Jamie held up his glass for a refill. When he realized the man was waiting to be paid, he blinked, and turned on the stool, and looked around the room as if he were waking from a bad dream. He was crying again when I paid the check.

I led him outside to the car. The night was still sticky and hot. I opened the door for him, and he got in and sat staring through the windshield, his hands folded in his lap. I backed the car out of the parking lot and began driving north. There was hardly any traffic at this hour of the night.

"Jamie," I said, "the police are going to check on where you went after you left that poker game. Are you sure it was The Innside Out?"

"I'm sure," he said.

"Because if you didn't go there . . ."

"That's where I went, Matt. Don't worry about it."

"Okay," I said.

"I should've gone straight home," he said.

"Don't start thinking that way, Jamie."

"I'm as much to blame as whoever . . ."

"No, you're not. Now quit it! You went to your usual poker game . . ."

"I left the game early . . ."

"You had no reason to believe anything would . . ."

"I should've gone home."

"You went for a drink instead, there's nothing wrong with that."

"You don't believe me, do you?" he said, and turned sharply on the seat.

"I do believe you, Jamie."

"Then why do you keep asking me where I went?"

"Only because the police . . ."

"The police never said a word about it. I told them where I went, and that was that. But my own lawyer . . ."

"Come on, Jamie. You can't believe they're not going to check. You left the poker game at a little before eleven, and you didn't get home till almost one. That's a gap of two hours. And the police *didn't* just let it pass. Ehrenberg asked how many drinks you'd had . . ."

"He was trying to find out if I was drunk. Down here, if you've had a drink . . ."

"No, it wasn't that. Because the *next* thing he did was ask how long you'd been at The Innside Out. Almost an hour and a half, you told him. From eleven to twelve-twenty. Only two drinks in all that time. *That's* what he was after, Jamie."

"Well, if I *had* only two drinks, was I supposed to lie and say I had *four?*"

"Of course not. I'm simply trying to tell you that Ehrenberg considers you a suspect. And he'll keep on thinking that way till he knows for sure just where you spent the time between eleven and one."

"I *told* him where I spent the time."

"Yes, and he's going to check it."

"I doubt if anyone'll remember me. The bar was crowded, I was . . ."

"At eleven on a Sunday night?"

"It's always crowded there, Matt."

"How do you know? Do you go there regularly?"

"I go there often enough. It's a good restaurant, they always get a crowd."

"Do you know the people that run it?"

"No."

"Do they know you?"

"I doubt it. They may, but I doubt it."

"Ehrenberg'll probably ask you for a picture, I'm second-guessing him now. He'll want something he can show the owners, and the bartender, the cashier, whoever was there. You give him a good one when he . . ."

"Why shouldn't I?"

"I keep telling you the man considers you a suspect, Jamie. You make sure you give him a good picture. I *want* somebody to remember your being there. Otherwise, he'll be back with a lot more questions."

"I'm not worried about that."

"Okay," I said.

"You keep saying okay, okay, but you keep circling back to it. Where the hell do you *think* I was, Matt?"

"Just where you said you were."

"Then why do you keep *asking* me where I was?"

"Because . . . look, Jamie, I'm not a cop, I'm a lawyer. And I know when somebody's evading a question. When Ehrenberg asked you if you or Maureen were fooling around outside the marriage, you didn't answer him. *He* may have missed that, but I didn't."

"I answered his question, Matt."

"No, you didn't. You sidestepped it. You said you were happily married, but you didn't answer the question."

"If I didn't answer it . . ."

"You didn't."

"It wasn't deliberate."

"Okay, it wasn't deliberate. Then would you like to answer it now? For me? Privately? For your lawyer who's trying to help?"

"I'll tell you anything you want to know."

"Okay. Straight out then. *Do* you have a girlfriend?"

"No."

"You said you were playing around in your former marriage . . ."

"Yes, but . . ."

"That can get to be a habit, Jamie."

"Not if you've changed your whole life for someone. Do you think I'd jeopardize a chance at happiness to . . . to fool around with—"

"That's what I'm asking you, Jamie."

"The answer is no."

"How about Maureen? Was there another man in her life?"

"No. I don't know. I don't think so. Look, you either trust someone completely, or you don't trust them at all."

"And you trusted her completely, is that right?"

"Yes, Matt. Completely."

"All right," I said.

I kept driving till I saw the first VACANCY sign. The place was called the Magnolia Garden Motel, small and hardly distinctive, but I doubted if we could do better without reservations at the height of the season.

"Will you be all right?" I asked.

"Yes," he said. "Thank you for everything, Matt."

"I'll call in the morning. If there's anything you need, even if it's just to talk, pick up the phone."

"Thank you," he said, and shook my hand.

I left him then and began driving home. A breeze was coming up as I crossed the bridge to Stone Crab Key. I kept wondering why I still didn't fully believe his story.

3

IT WAS a little after three A.M. when I got to the house. I went directly into the den, turned on the desk lamp, and phoned my partner Frank. When I told him what had happened, the first thing he said was "Oh, God" and then he asked if Jamie had committed the murders. I told him Jamie had said no, and then filled him in on everything else he'd said. Frank advised me to go to bed, he'd see me in the morning. We said good night, and I hung up, and sat at the desk for a moment, unmoving, my hand on the telephone receiver. I snapped off the lamp then, and rose, and went down the hall to the bedroom.

Susan was asleep.

I tiptoed into the room and then went into the bathroom to turn on the light, leaving the door cracked so that light slanted into the room but did not touch the bed. I had no desire to awaken her. We'd been fighting when the call from Jamie came. I had, in fact, been on the verge of asking her for a divorce.

The fight had started twelve hours earlier, on our way to the Virginia Slims finals that afternoon. The matches were supposed to begin at one o'clock, and we'd left the house at twenty to, which was cutting it a bit close on a

Sunday at the height of the tourist season. There are only two seasons in Calusa: the tourist season and summer. In the good old summertime, there is no one here but mad dogs and Englishmen. And me. During the season, most of the tourists come from the Midwest. That's because if you draw a line due south from Columbus, Ohio, it will go straight through the middle of Calusa. Frank says that Calusa is really only Michigan on the Gulf of Mexico. Maybe he's right.

The fight began because my daughter Joanna asked a question as we were crossing the Cortez Causeway. I was at the wheel, and I was driving Susan's car as opposed to my car. Susan is an only child. Only children are very specific about what is theirs and what is yours. The Mercedes-Benz was Susan's. The Karmann Ghia was mine. Susan was very jealous of her possessions, and especially of the Mercedes-Benz which—I don't mind telling you—had cost seventeen thousand dollars and some change.

At precisely 12:47 P.M. on the dashboard clock (I remember looking at it because I knew we were running late and I didn't know whether the Evert-Goolagong match would be the first one, and I didn't want to miss the opening serve) my daughter Joanna asked whether it was absolutely necessary for her to go with us that night to hear Mstislav Rostropovich. Calusa is a very cultural town. Not for nothing is it called the Athens of Florida. Actually, no one calls it that but Frank. He's originally from New York. When he calls Calusa the Athens of Florida, his eyes glint and his lip curls.

"Rostropovich is the world's greatest cello player," I told Joanna.

"You took me to see the world's greatest *violin* player, too," Joanna said, "and *he* put me to sleep."

I did not blame that on Isaac Stern. When a person is twelve years old, anything but reruns of *I Love Lucy* will put her to sleep. Besides, Mr. Stern was working against a rolling and continuous wave of coughs, sneezes and snorts that caused him first to change his program mid-concert, and then to chide the audience gently for the epidemic of nasal catarrh. When we left the auditorium that night, I ventured the guess that we wouldn't be seeing Mr. Stern in Calusa again. Susan said, "Why not?"

I said, "Because the codgers were rude."

"It's rude of *you* to call them codgers all the time," Susan said. "They're simply old people."

"They're *rude* old people," I said. "I'd personally rather choke than cough in the middle of a violin passage."

"I personally wish you would," Susan said.

It was perhaps memory of the Isaac Stern argument that prompted the Virginia Slims argument. In recent months, I'd taken to cataloging our many and varied arguments, the better to recall them fondly. I did not know, of course, that the Virginia Slims argument would later become the Beefeater Martini argument and still later the Reginald Soames argument and eventually what I will always and forever remember as the Jamie Purchase argument, even though his phone call at one in the morning ended all argument at once. It was still not yet one in the afternoon when Susan said, "Would you mind not discussing this now?"

"Discussing what?" I said.

"Whether or not Joanna has to come with us tonight. We're late as it is . . ."

"We're not *that* late," I said.

"Well, just keep your eyes on the road, okay?"

"There's nothing I can do but stay in line, anyway," I said. "This car may have cost seventeen thousand dollars but it doesn't have wings."

"*And* some change," Susan said. "You forgot to say 'and some change.' "

"And some change," I said.

"Just drive," she said, "okay?"

"No, *you* just drive," I said, and pulled up the hand brake at the stoplight on U.S. 41, and got out of the car and came around to the other side of it. I slammed the door when I got in again.

"I don't know what *you're* so angry about," Susan said.

"I'm not angry," I said. "If you don't like the way I drive, you can drive yourself. It's as simple as that."

"I don't like to drive when I have the curse," Susan said. She was thirty-two years old, and she still referred to her menstrual cycle as "the curse." I think she felt the words implied intercourse denied, the curse being not the flow of blood itself, but rather the interruption it caused in an otherwise wild and passionate sex life. There was, in fact, a look of suppressed sensuality about Susan. Dark brooding eyes, an oval face framed by cascades of long brown hair that fell straight and loose to her shoulders, a full pouting mouth that gave an impression—not entirely inaccurate—of a sullen, spoiled defiant beauty.

We got home from the matches at about five-thirty. Susan had sulked for most of the afternoon, but she seemed to have got over her peeve by the time she'd showered and dressed for dinner. It was decided that if Joanna could not appreciate the better things in life, why then she could stay home.

She said, "Good, I can watch *The Sound of Music* on television."

"If you came with us," I said, "you could *hear* the sound of music in person."

The Beefeater Martini argument started when I ordered my second drink before dinner.

"You're not going to have *two* of those, are you?" Susan asked.

"Yes," I said, "I'm going to have two of them."

"You know how you get after two martinis."

"How do I get?"

"Fuzzy."

It was Susan's contention that I never got drunk when I drank, for example, two Scotches with soda or two *anythings* with soda, but I always got drunk or fuzzy or furry or slurry (these were all Susan's words) when I had two martinis, especially two *Beefeater* martinis, the magic word Beefeater somehow adding more potency to the drink.

"Susan," I said, "please let's enjoy dinner without another argument."

"We wouldn't argue if you wouldn't drink," Susan said.

"We argued this afternoon," I said, "and I wasn't drinking."

"You probably had one before we left the house."

"Susan, you *know* I didn't have one before we left the house. What are you trying to establish here? That I'm—"

"Then why'd you get all upset when all I did was tell you to watch the road instead of—"

"I got upset because Joanna had asked me a question, and I was trying—"

"That was no reason for you to snap at me."

"I snapped at you because you were nagging. And you're nagging now. If a man has a couple of martinis before dinner—"

"*Beef*eater martinis," she said.

"Yes, Beefeater martinis, right, that doesn't make him an alcoholic."

"You're going to get fuzzy and spoil the evening," Susan said.

"The evening is spoiled already," I answered.

Susan fell asleep while Rostropovich was playing Schumann's *Funf Stucke im Volkston,* Opus 102, *Mit Humor,* no less. I said nothing about it. We had not exchanged a word since leaving the restaurant, and we said nothing on the way home, either. Joanna was still awake when we came in. It was already a half-hour past her normal bedtime. "It's ten-thirty," I said, tapping my watch.

"I know," she said.

"Have you finished your homework?"

"Yeah," she said, "but I was trying to figure out this record club thing."

"What record club thing?"

"The *record* club, Dad. My *record* club."

"Oh, yes," I said, "your record club."

"Will you help me fill out the dingus?"

"Tomorrow," I said.

"Dad, it's due back on the sixth."

She went into her room and came back with a printed card. I studied it carefully and handed it back to her. "It only has to be *postmarked* the sixth," I said.

"Where does it say that?"

"Right there."

Joanna looked at the card. "Oh," she said. "Yeah, that's right."

"Tomorrow's only the first. We've got plenty of time."

"Okay, Dad," she said, and kissed me good night. "Mom?" she said.

"Yes?" Susan said.

"G'night, Mom."

"Good night," Susan said. She was already in bed. Joanna went to the bed, and bent over and kissed her on the cheek.

"G'night," she said again, and then went to her own room.

I undressed silently, and turned out the light on my side of the bed. Susan lay stiffly beside me. I knew she was not asleep, her breathing was too erratic, interrupted by occasional long sighs. At last, she said, "What is it, Matthew?"

"What do you mean, what is it?"

"Why do we fight so much?"

"You invariably start them, Susan."

"That isn't true."

"You started the fight on the way to the tennis—"

"No, you flew off the handle."

"Because you were bugging me about the way I was driving."

"You said you didn't want to be late."

"We were in no danger of being late."

"There was a lot of traffic, and you weren't watching the road, you were talking to Joanna."

"Here we go again."

"It's true, Matthew. You get distracted, and you don't know what you're doing."

"Susan, you make me sound like someone who can't tie his own shoelaces!"

"I don't want another argument."

"Then cut it out, would you please? I *can't* hold a conversation and drive at the same time, I *can't* drink two martinis before dinner, I *can't* . . . ."

"You *do* drink too much."

"When is the last time . . . would you please tell me the last time . . . can you tell me *any*time you've seen me falling-down drunk or even . . ."

"You get fuzzy," Susan said.

"Susan, I drink less than almost any man I know. Old Reggie next door—"

"Mr. Soames is a drunk."

"That's exactly my point. *I* am *not* a drunk, I am not even a heavy drinker. What is this, would you please tell me? Is this *Gaslight* or something? Are you trying to convince me I'm a drunk because I have two martinis before dinner? Are you trying to *drive* me to drink, Susan, is that it? Susan, *you* had two drinks before dinner, do you know that? You had two drinks, Susan, I counted them. You had two Manhattans, Susan. You fell asleep during the concert—"

"I did not fall asleep," she said. "And please don't change the subject."

"Susan, say it, okay? Do you think I'm a drunk? Say it."

"I do not think you're a drunk."

"Fine, then . . ."

"But I *do* think you drink too much."

"*What,* exactly, is too much, Susan?"

"Two Beefeater martinis is too much."

"Jesus Christ!" I said.

"Lower your voice," she said. "All the windows are open."

"Then close the windows and turn on the air conditioner," I said.

"The air conditioner is broken," she said. "Or did you forget *that,* too?"

"That's right, I have a very poor memory," I said. "That's why I'm such a lousy lawyer. I can't remember what a witness is saying from one minute to the next."

"No one said you're a lousy lawyer."

"No, but I have a lousy memory."

"You forgot about the air conditioner, didn't you?"

"I thought you called about the air conditioner."

"I called, but they wouldn't come on a Sunday. If you paid more attention to what was going on around here, you'd have known nobody came to fix it."

"I thought they came while I was out getting the *Times*."

"Then why would we have all the windows open instead of the air conditioner on? If the air conditioner had been fixed . . ."

"How do I know? Maybe you want Old Reggie to hear

us fighting. Maybe you want him to suffer a coronary occlusion."

"I hate the way you talk about Mr. Soames. He's a nice man."

"He's a fart," I said, and got out of bed and stalked into the living room.

I debated putting on the Modern Jazz Quartet. I sometimes played the Modern Jazz Quartet at full volume just to annoy Old Reggie next door. Reggie had a cavalry mustache. He carried a walking stick, which he poked at lizards. He also poked it at our cat, Sebastian. Sebastian was a much finer individual than Reginald Soames. Whenever I played the Modern Jazz Quartet at full volume, Sebastian the cat stretched out on the terrazzo floor in the living room, exactly midway between the two speakers. He closed his eyes. His ears twitched in time to the beat. He was a most appreciative and big pussycat. Old Reggie was a fart. When I played the Modern Jazz Quartet—I didn't even *like* the Modern Jazz Quartet, I only played it to annoy Old Reggie—he came out with his walking stick and said in his whiskey-seared voice, "A bit loud, eh, Junior?" and then he said, "What *is* that crap, anyway?" I always told him it was Mozart. "Mozart?" he said. "Mozart, eh?"

I realized all at once that Reginald Soames was a sad and harmless old man who simply had the ill fortune of living next door to someone whose marriage was in trouble. I thought about that. I thought about the only two things in this marriage that meant anything to me—my daughter Joanna and Sebastian the cat. I was on my way back to the bedroom to tell Susan everything, to tell her at last, to tell her I wanted a divorce, to tell her she could have the house and both cars and the boat and the savings account and the record collection and the piano nobody played if only she would let me take Joanna and the cat with me when I left.

That was when the telephone rang.

It was Jamie Purchase calling to say his wife and two children had been brutally murdered.

Now, at a little past three in the morning, as I pulled back the sheet on my side of the bed and got in beside

Susan, my only wish was that she would not wake up. I was exhausted, I was numb, I didn't know what I was feeling or thinking. Before the argument, before the call from Jamie, I had set the alarm for seven A.M. At eight every Monday I played tennis with Mark Goldman, who was a dozen years older than I and a dozen light-years better. Seven A.M. was only four hours away. I tried to figure out a plan of action. Should I call Mark at three in the morning to tell him I couldn't play tennis with him tomorrow? Should I leave the alarm set for seven and call him when I woke up? Or should I simply turn off the alarm and sleep till Mark called me from the club to ask where the hell I was? I was too tired to think. I left the alarm set for seven. Cautiously, I eased my legs under the sheet. I had the dread premonition that if Susan woke up the first thing she'd say would be, "And *another* thing . . ."

She stirred beside me. She rolled into my arms. We were both naked, we had slept naked from the beginning, thirteen years ago. The end had almost come two hours ago, when I'd been about to tell her everything. Her body was warm with sleep. She put her hand on my right shoulder. I had known this woman since she was seventeen. I had married her when she was nineteen. I was now ready to divorce her. I had not yet told her, but I was ready.

4

I WAS awake at six-thirty, listening to a cardinal chirping out back. I got out of bed without waking Susan, put on a robe, and went into the kitchen. Joanna was sitting at the table, spooning cornflakes into her mouth, reading the newspaper.

I knew better than to talk to her while she was reading. Or for that matter, while she was eating breakfast. Joanna is not a morning person. The only time I could get away with talking to her before nine A.M. was when she was still an infant. Susan and I used to take turns getting up for the early-morning feeding. I'd hold Joanna in my arms and whisper sweet nonsense into her round little face while she gulped down formula that was surely inedible. Her eating habits hadn't changed much. She liked her cornflakes soggy, she shoveled dripping spoonfuls of them into her mouth blindly, her eyes on the latest adventures of *Hägar the Horrible*. "Good morning," I said, and she said, "Uhh." I went to the refrigerator and took out the plastic container of orange juice.

I had picked and squeezed the oranges myself the day before. Old Reggie saw me picking them and asked whether I intended to squeeze the whole batch. I told him that's what I was intending, yes. He said it was best to squeeze only what I'd be using immediately. That was the way to get the most benefit from them, and besides juice tasted better when it was squoze fresh. That was the word he used: squoze. I told him I didn't have time to squeeze fresh juice every morning. I told him I tried to pick and squeeze enough oranges on Saturday or Sunday to last me through the week. Old Reggie shook his head and poked his cane at a lizard. The next time I saw him, I would have to apologize to him. Not for squeezing more oranges than I could immediately use, and not for the Modern Jazz Quartet either. Only for taking out on him all the things that were troubling me.

"What was all the excitement last night?" Joanna asked.

At first I thought she meant the fight between Susan and me. She'd undoubtedly heard us railing at each other. Then I realized she was talking about the phone ringing at a quarter to one, and my leaving the house shortly afterward. I didn't know quite what to say. How do you tell a twelve-year-old that three people she knew and possibly loved had been stabbed to death the night before?

"Dad?" she said. "What was it? Why'd you leave the house that way?"

"Dr. Purchase called me," I said.

"What about?"

I took a deep breath. "Somebody killed Maureen and the little girls."

She put down her spoon. She looked at me.

"Who?" she said.

"They don't know yet."

"Wow," she said.

"You'd better get dressed, huh?"

"I've got time," she said, and glanced at the wall clock, and said immediately, "No, I haven't," and got up and ran for her bedroom. I put up a kettle of water to boil, and then I sat down at the table and sipped my juice and studied the newspaper. It made no mention of the murders. There were going to be renewed SALT talks. A governor in a nearby state had been accused of larceny. A Hollywood celebrity had played tennis at the Field Club on Sunday morning. Chris Evert had won the Virginia Slims singles tournament and Governor Askew had declared yesterday

Chris Evert Day in honor of—should I keep my tennis date?

The water was boiling.

I fixed myself a cup of instant coffee, and then carried it outside to where a dozen small docks jutted out into the canal shared by the houses on both sides of it. The sun was just coming up. The wind of the night before had blown away whatever had been hanging over the city and smothering it; the day was going to be bright and clear. I crossed the lawn, greener here than out front, wet with early morning dew. *The Windbag* was tied fore and aft to the dock, one of her halyards banging against the aluminum mast and setting up a terrible racket. I climbed aboard and tightened the line, and the clanging stopped abruptly. I had named the boat over Susan's protests; she had cost seven thousand dollars used, which was not bad for a twenty-five-footer that slept four comfortably. The water in the canal was still. Down the street, I heard an automobile start. I looked at my watch. It was fifteen minutes to seven. The city of Calusa was coming awake.

I went inside the house, and then on through to the bedroom. Susan was still asleep, her hair fanned out over the pillow, her right arm bent at the elbow, the palm facing the ceiling. The sheet was tangled between her legs. I pushed in the alarm button on the back of the clock. Across the hall, Joanna was showering. I could hear the steady drumming of the water. The radio was on in her bedroom, her usual rock and roll station. She turned it on very softly each morning, the moment she got out of bed. It was as if she could not bear being without music at any time during her waking hours. I sometimes wished she would turn it on loud instead. This way, I could only hear the monotonous sound of the bass guitar, without even a hint of the melody.

I felt well rested, but I didn't know what demands might be made on me later in the day, and I had the feeling I should be getting to the office instead of the Calusa Tennis Club. At the same time, I didn't imagine Jamie would be up and around much before noon, and I could see no reason to be sitting at my desk at nine sharp, waiting for a call. I would, in any event, be at the office no later than nine-thirty, ten o'clock. I decided to keep the date, went into the bathroom I shared with Susan, took off my robe, and turned on the shower. As I lathered myself with soap Susan had bought on our trip to England the summer before, the soap she warned me constantly not to leave in the dish since it melted so fast and was so awfully expensive, as I watched rivulets of foam run over my chest, my belly and my groin, I thought only of Aggie.

The Calusa Tennis Club had been undergoing alterations for the past six or seven months and was finally nearing completion. It promised to be even larger and grander than before, but meanwhile there was lumber stacked everywhere, and kegs of nails, and rolls of tar paper, and sawhorses marking off areas that were not to be trespassed while construction was under way. Mark Goldman was sitting on one such sawhorse, or rather leaning against it, his right ankle crossed over his left, his racket resting on his partial lap. He looked at his watch the moment he saw me.

"Thought you'd never get here," he said.

Every time he said that, I automatically looked at my own watch. He said it every Monday morning. I had looked at the dashboard clock before getting out of the car, and it had read three minutes to eight. I had checked my own watch as I crossed the parking lot and the time then was *two* minutes to eight. But now, as Mark said what he said every Monday morning since we'd begun our game together, I looked at my watch like a damn fool.

Mark had curly black hair and dark brown eyes and a mustache he'd begun cultivating only two months back. When he started growing it, he told me mustaches were the thing. He said mustaches drove young girls wild. This was important to Mark because he was forty-eight years old and a bachelor. If he could not drive young girls wild, then whom was he *supposed* to drive wild—old ladies of thirty-nine or forty? No, no. He had been a successful bachelor all these years only because he watched the trends. "Trends, Matt," he said. "You want to succeed in anything, you've got to watch the trends. Mustaches are a trend right now. There isn't a girl under thirty who will even *spit* on a man without a mustache."

"Will they spit on a man *with* a mustache?" I asked.

"Nobody likes a smartass, Matt," he said, and cocked his finger at me.

He destroyed me.

Instead of taking pity on a man who was sporting a highly visible Ace bandage on his right wrist, he instead played better than I'd ever seen him play. His serves were devastating. The ball came in low over the net and then hit the court and bounced up high and away to the left, curving into my backhand. Because of my tennis elbow, I couldn't follow through without wincing in pain. Most of my returns were weak little shots that popped the ball high up into the air to be met on the other side of the net by Mark's overhead smash. When I did manage to return a serve with something more respectable, Mark dazzled me with a repertoire of cross-court slashes, dinky dropshots, infuriating lobs and vicious volleys designed to take off my head if I had the audacity to step into their path. He won the first set 6–2, and the second 6–0. When he asked if I wanted to play a third, I told him he was a cruel and heartless bastard who took advantage of cripples.

"You're wearing the bandage in the wrong place," he said. "If your elbow hurts, you should wear it on your elbow, not your wrist."

"No," I said, "it's the action of the wrist that causes the pain in the elbow."

"Who told you that?"

"My doctor."

"What doctor?"

"Dr. Cooper, he's an orthopedist."

"He doesn't know tennis elbows," Mark said. "I had my first tennis elbow when I was sixteen."

"What'd you do for it?"

"I wrapped it in a bandage and went up on the roof with a girl named Giselle. Giselle knew how to fix a tennis elbow, all right. If Giselle was here in Calusa, she'd fix that tennis elbow of yours in a minute."

"It's not the elbow, it's really the wrist."

"She'd fix your wrist, too, old Giselle."

It was twenty minutes past nine. Mark's exercise in demolition had taken little more than an hour. Where the courts had earlier been filled almost exclusively with men, there were now women beginning to play, or walking along the shrub-lined paths toward unoccupied courts. Some of the courts were being watered, and there was the whispering sound of the sprinklers and above that the steady rhythmic sound of balls being hit and returned, hit and returned. The morning was cool, a faint breeze rustled in the trees surrounding the courts. It occurred to me that something was different. Or rather . . . *nothing* was different, that was the trouble. Everything was the same.

This could have been Monday morning last week or the week before. There was no excited buzz in the air, no seeming knowledge of the fact that last night, not too many miles from here, a woman and her two daughters had been stabbed to death. True enough, there were sometimes fatal stabbings or shootings in Calusa, but these were normally the result of barroom brawls that got out of hand. It was rare that we had a sensational murder. The only one I could remember in the three years I'd been living here had taken place on Stone Crab Key—the Howell murder case. The reverberations of that one had rumbled through the city for months. This morning, it seemed the only people who yet knew anything at all about the murders on Jacaranda Drive were the ones who'd been at Jamie's house last night. I was suddenly chilled; one of those people was the murderer.

"The reason tennis has become such a popular sport," Mark said, "is that it gives women a legal opportunity to show their panties. If women had to play tennis in long dresses, they'd suddenly take up quilting. But the way it is now, a woman reaches up to serve, she bends over to receive, the whole world can see her panties and comment on her beautiful ass. It's wonderful. Do you have time for coffee, counselor, or must you go plead the Sacco-Vanzetti case?"

"I have time for coffee," I said.

There were half a dozen men and four women sitting at tables inside the screened-in coffee shop. Mark looked the women over as we went to the counter. One of the women, a busty blonde wearing a white T-shirt and very short shorts blatantly looked him over in return. He winked at her, and she turned away and began an overly animated conversation with the woman sitting on her right. Mark ordered two coffees, and asked if I wanted a cheese Danish. I said I'd skip the Danish. We took a table just inside the screen, overlooking court number five. Two very strong women players were playing singles on it. One of them appeared to be in her late sixties, but she had a serve that was giving her younger opponent a lot of trouble. I watched them in silence for several moments, sipping my coffee, savoring it. Mark's attention was on the blonde who'd earlier appraised him. When I asked him what he'd been doing lately, he missed the question. I repeated it.

"Professionally or socially?" he asked. "Never mind, the hell with professionally. Socially's more interesting. Do you remember my telling you about a young lady named Eileen?"

"Yes, the National Airlines stewardess."

"No that was Arlene."

"I don't remember anyone named Eileen."

"Anyway, we've become very friendly."

"Good," I said.

"Not so good," Mark said. "She's moving back to Ohio. She's had an offer to teach at Oberlin. She called me last night, said she desperately had to see me. I told her I couldn't. She said, 'But I'm leaving for *Ohio!*' I said, 'I *know* you're leaving for Ohio, honey, but that's not till September. This isn't even *March* yet.' "

"So did you go see her?"

"No, I couldn't, I had a poker game. Your friend's game."

I looked at him. "My friend's game?"

"Jamie Bircher. You introduced me to him once a long time ago. At Marina Blue."

"Purchase, do you mean? Jamie Purchase?"

"Yeah. An internist or something?"

"You played poker with him last night?"

"Well, don't sound so shocked, Matt. It's perfectly legal, you know."

"Yes, I know, I just . . ."

"Didn't remember me from a hole in the wall. Shook hands, how do you do, Mr. Goldman, sat down and started counting his chips." Mark shrugged. "Hell with him," he said.

"I don't understand," I said. "Are you a regular in the game?"

"No, no, a friend of mine called yesterday afternoon—ten minutes before Eileen did, as a matter of fact. Art Kramer, do you know him? He sells real estate out on Whisper."

"No, I don't know him."

"Two of his players had dropped out, he asked if I'd do him a favor and play. I played in the game once a long time ago. I didn't much like it, so I never went back. They don't play any wild games, just five-card draw or seven-card . . . do you play poker?"

"Yes."

"Art *doesn't*. Not really. He loves the game, but he can't play it to save his ass. You know how much he lost last night?"

"How much?"

"Forty dollars. I know that doesn't sound like much, but these guys play for nickels and dimes. Your friend walked out with a bundle."

"My friend?"

"Tell me, Matt, has your tennis elbow moved up into your ear?"

"You mean Jamie Purchase?"

"Yes, your friend. Jamie Purchase your friend. Jamie Purchase the internist. Ask him to take a look at your ear, Matt."

"You mean he won?"

"Yes. Very good, Matt. That's exactly what I meant when I said he walked out with a bundle. He won. Excellent, Matt, you're doing very—"

"No, wait a minute. He won? He *won?*"

"Must be an echo in this place," Mark said. "Yes, he won. Or to put it yet another way, he won, yes. Cashed in his chips, said good night and walked out."

"Did he say why he was leaving?"

"He was tired, poor fellow. Said he had to go home and get some sleep."

"He said he was going home?"

Mark looked at me. "I feel certain I'm speaking English," he said, "but . . ."

"Mark, did he actually *say* he was going home?"

"Yes, he actually *said* he was going home. Not a very nice thing to do, Matt. You don't walk out of a game when you're winning. We played till one o'clock, but he'd already taken sixty bucks out of the game by eleven."

"Is that when he left? Eleven?"

"A little before eleven, in fact." Mark shook his head. "It wasn't the first time, either. According to Art, your friend makes a habit of it."

"Of what? Leaving the game early?"

"Yeah."

"When he's winning, do you mean?"

"Even when he's losing. Art likes to have seven players in the game, keeps it lively. When somebody leaves the game early it changes the dynamics. I'll bet Art tries to ease him out. He was mad as hell last night, I can tell you that." Mark paused. "What'll your friend do then? Without the poker game for his alibi?"

"Well . . . I don't know what you mean."

"Don't you? It's plain as day, Matt. Your friend's got a little something going on the side. Listen, more power to him. But can't he find a better alibi than a poker game? I mean, can't he at least go perform an appendectomy every Sunday night?"

5

I SPENT the next ten minutes in a telephone booth outside a gasoline station. The traffic at a quarter to ten had thickened considerably, automobiles and trucks moving bumper to bumper in both directions. For as long as I'd been living here, there'd been talk of financing an interstate superhighway that would divert traffic away from the city and ease the burden on U.S. 41. They were still talking about it. The talk said that even if they started building it this very minute, it wouldn't be ready for ten years. By that time, the line of traffic on the Trail would be frozen solid from Tampa all the way down to the Everglades.

I called Aggie first.

The phone rang three times before she answered it.

"Hello?" she said.

"Hi."

"Matt, good! I was just getting ready to leave the house."

"Where are you going?"

"I've got a dumb rehearsal. Is there any possibility you can get away this afternoon?"

"Why?"

"Julie's got a guitar lesson, and Gerry's got basketball

practice. They're both being picked up, I'll be free till at least five."

"Don't tempt me."

"Let me tempt you."

"I'm not sure," I said. "From the way it looks now, I may not even be able to *call* you later."

"Why not?" she asked at once. "Is something wrong?"

"Jamie Purchase's wife and kids were murdered last night."

"You're joking!"

"No, honey, I wish I—"

"Oh, Matt, how awful. Do they know who did it?"

"Not yet."

"It wasn't Jamie, was it?"

"I don't think so."

"But you're not sure."

"I just don't know, Aggie."

"What do the police think?"

"A man named Ehrenberg's in charge of the investigation. He said Jamie's not a suspect, but I'm not sure I believe him."

"What'd Jamie tell you?"

"That he didn't do it. Honey, I've got to go. What time will you be through with that rehearsal?"

"One at the very latest."

"I'll try to call you after that. Aggie . . . ?"

"Yes, darling?"

"I almost told her last night. I almost told Susan I wanted a divorce."

"But you didn't."

"No."

"All right, darling."

"Aggie, I love you."

"I love you, too."

"I'll try to call later."

"Yes."

"I love you," I said, and put the phone gently back on the cradle. I fished another dime from my pocket, looked up the number for the Magnolia Garden Motel, and quickly dialed it.

"Magnolia Garden," a woman said, "good morning."

"Good morning," I said. "May I please speak to Dr. Purchase, he's in room number twelve."

"Unit number twelve, yes, sir," she said. "Dr. Purchase, Dr. Purchase . . ." Her voice trailed. I had the feeling she was running her index finger down a list of guests. "He's checked out, sir," she said.

"Are you sure?"

"Yes, sir."

"When did he leave?"

"About nine, I guess it was. Calusa Cab picked him up."

"Thank you," I said, and hung up. It was very hot in the phone booth. I opened the door to let in some air. A trailer truck was rumbling past, it filled the booth with noise and Diesel exhaust. I knew from experience that taxicab companies, in Calusa or anywhere else, would tell no one but the police where they had driven a passenger. I debated calling Calusa Cab and saying I was Detective Ehrenberg. I didn't have the nerve. Instead, I tried to figure where Jamie might have gone at nine in the morning, still dressed in what he was wearing the night before—he'd taken nothing with him when we left the house. Not even a shaving kit. I figured the only place he could have gone was back home to shower and shave and change his clothes. I knew the number by heart.

"Detective Di Luca," a voice said. Ehrenberg's partner, the small dark man with the blue eyes. His voice was rather high-pitched. It came as a surprise. I'd have expected from him something closer to a rasp or a whisper.

"This is Matthew Hope," I said. "I'm Dr. Purchase's attorney."

"Yes, sir, good morning," Di Luca said.

"Good morning. I was wondering if Dr. Purchase might be there."

"Yes, sir, he got here just a little while ago. Did you want to speak to him?"

"If I may."

"Well . . . just a second, okay?"

He put down the phone. I heard him yelling something to somebody named Harry. I caught the word "doctor," and then Jamie came on the line.

"Hello?" he said.

"Jamie, this is Matt. Listen to me. I want to see you right away, and not at the house with policemen crawling all over the place."

"What's wrong, Matt?"

"Nothing's wrong, I have to talk to you. How nearly dressed are you?"

"I'm dressed."

"Had you planned on working today?"

"No. I've already called in and told Louise to cancel my appointments."

"Good. Can you get to my office by ten-thirty?"

"What is it, Matt?"

"Can you get there?"

"Yes, sure."

"I'll see you then," I said. "Good-bye, Jamie."

"Good-bye, Matt," he said. His voice seemed puzzled.

I put the receiver back onto the hook and went out to where I'd parked the car near the air hose. The garage attendant was standing there with his hands on his hips. He seemed offended about something; I guessed I was blocking his hose. He kept watching me as I climbed into the car. Just as I started to back out, he said, "How much you want for that car?"

"It's not for sale," I said.

"You ought to get that fender fixed," he said. "Ruins the look of it."

"I'll get around to it."

"They don't make those cars no more, you know."

"I know," I said. "It's a classic."

"Damn right, it is," he said.

The day was beginning to warm up. I turned on the air conditioner. It rattled and clonked and clunked, but it cooled off the automobile. It was almost ten o'clock when I reached the cutoff to Route 74. I switched on the radio and caught the last few bars of a schmaltzy arrangement of "Sunrise, Sunset." The news came on immediately afterward. The lead story was the murder of Maureen Purchase and her daughters Emily and Eve.

It was real at last.

Cynthia Huellen was a native Floridian with long blonde hair and a glorious tan that she worked at almost fanatically; never a weekend went by that did not find Cynthia on a beach or a boat. She was easily the most beautiful person in the law offices of Summerville & Hope, twenty-three years old, and employed by us as a receptionist. We kept telling her to quit the job and go to law school instead. She already had a B.A. from the University of South Florida, and we were ready to take her into the firm the minute she passed her bar exams. Cynthia just grinned and said, "No, I don't want the hassle of school again."

She looked up as I came into the office.

"Frank would like to see you right away," she said.

"Okay. Any calls?"

"Mr. Galatier."

"What'd he want?"

"Said to remind you of his appointment at twelve."

"How could I forget? Anybody else?"

"Your wife. Said it wasn't important."

"Okay. Buzz Frank and tell him I'm going to shower and change. I'll be with him in five minutes. Tell him Jamie's coming in at ten-thirty."

"What an awful, awful thing," Cynthia said.

"Yes. And Cyn, I think maybe you'd better call Galatier and tell him I can't see him after all. It's liable to get hectic around here, and I won't need a goddamn lunatic underfoot."

"Did you win?" Cynthia asked.

"No," I answered.

The one luxury I'd insisted on in our offices was a shower stall. The architect wanted to put it on the wall between my office and Frank's, next door to the bathroom, where the plumbing was going to be. But he couldn't do this without cutting down on the interior size of Frank's office. Frank said he did not mind people taking showers in the office when they should have been taking them at home. He did, however, mind his office being trimmed to the size of a broom closet simply to accommodate a sweaty athlete. Our architect had opted for the other side of the corridor instead, putting the shower stall between the conference room and Karl Jennings' office—Karl was just out of law school and enjoyed no executive privileges. I went into my own office, picked up my change of clothes, and was starting toward the door again when the telephone rang. I put everything down on the leather couch opposite the desk and picked up the phone.

"Yes?" I said.

"Mr. Hope, it's your wife again," Cynthia said. "Can you talk to her now?"

"All right, put her on," I said. I looked at my watch. It was almost ten past ten; Jamie would be here in twenty minutes and I still hadn't talked to Frank.

"Hello?" Susan said.

"Yes, Susan, what is it?"

"Are you still angry?" she asked.

"No, just in a hurry."

"I'm sorry about yesterday."

"That's all right," I said. "Susan, I really can't talk right now. We'll discuss it when I get home, okay?"

"You haven't forgotten tonight, have you?"

"What's tonight?"

"The gallery opening, and then dinner at—"

"Yes, right. It's here on my calendar. Susan, I've got to say good-bye now."

"All right, we'll talk when you get home."

"Fine."

"Do you have any idea what time that'll be?"

"Susan, I just *got* here this minute, I haven't even—"

"All right, darling, go ahead," she said.

"We'll talk later," I said.

"Yes, good-bye."

"Good-bye," I said and put down the receiver and collected my clothes again. I was carrying them across the corridor when Frank stepped out of his office next door.

There are people who say that Frank and I look alike. I cannot see any resemblance. I'm six feet two inches tall and weigh a hundred and ninety pounds. Frank's a half-inch under six feet, and he weighs a hundred and seventy, which he watches like a hawk. We both have dark hair and brown eyes, but Frank's face is rounder than mine. Frank says there are only two types of faces in the world—pig faces and fox faces. He classifies himself as a pig face and me as a fox face. There is nothing derogatory about either label; they are only intended to be descriptive. Frank first told me about his designation system last October. Ever since, I've been unable to look at anyone without automatically categorizing him as either pig or fox.

"Why's Jamie coming here?" he said at once.

"I asked him to. He was lying about that poker game, Frank. He was winning when he left."

"Who says?"

"Mark Goldman was in the same game."

"Then why'd Jamie say he was losing?"

"That's what I want to ask him. That's why he's coming here."

Jamie came into the office fifteen minutes later. He looked well rested, well scrubbed and cleanly shaved. He was wearing a white linen leisure suit, dark blue sports shirt open at the throat. Frank took his hand and expressed sincere condolences. I asked Jamie if he wanted a drink, and he looked at his watch, and then shook his head. I looked at Frank. Frank nodded.

"Jamie," I said, "we're your lawyers, and we've got to ask you the same questions the police are going to ask. And we need the answers before they get them."

"Okay," Jamie said. There was the same puzzled tone in his voice that had been there earlier on the telephone.

"I'll give it to you straight," I said. "I'm not trying to trick you into anything, I'm asking only for the truth. A man named Mark Goldman was in that poker game with you last night. You'd met him before, I'd introduced you one day when we were having lunch at Marina Blue. I guess you'd forgotten him, you didn't seem to recognize him last night. Man with a mustache, about your height . . ."

"What about him?" Jamie said.

"I played tennis with him this morning. He told me you were winning when you left the game. Is that true?"

"No, I was losing," Jamie said.

"How *much* were you losing?" Frank asked.

"Thirty, forty dollars."

"So you decided to go home."

"Yes."

"But instead you went to The Innside Out for a drink. How come?"

"I was feeling low. About losing."

"About losing," Frank repeated.

"Yes."

"Jamie," I said, "Detective Ehrenberg is going to talk to all the players who were in that game last night. That's why he took their names from you. He'll eventually get to Mark Goldman, even though he was one of the players whose names you didn't know. Mark's going to tell him exactly what he told me. You were winning when you quit. You were tired. You were going home to sleep. Now unless you can *prove* you were at The Innside Out, Ehrenberg's going to think you *did* go home. He's going to think you got there a lot earlier than a quarter to one, when you called me. He's going to think you were maybe there in time to murder Maureen and the kids. Now Jamie . . ."

"I *didn't* murder them."

"Did you go directly home from that poker game?"

"No. I *told* you where I went. I went to the Innside Out."

"Jamie, we're talking about first-degree murder here," Frank said. "We're talking about the death penalty."

"I didn't kill anybody."

"*Were* you winning when you left the game?"

"What difference does it make?"

"If you were winning, the other players'll tell that to the police. And the police'll wonder why you *later* said you were losing. So which was it, Jamie? Were you winning, or were—"

"I was winning."

"All right. Then why'd you leave the game?"

"I was tired. It was just what I said. I wanted to go home to sleep."

"But instead you went to The Innside Out."

"Yes."

"I don't believe you," I said.

"Was it a woman?" Frank asked.

"No."

"*Was* it?" he insisted.

"Oh, Jesus," Jamie said, and buried his face in his hands.

"Tell us," I said.

He began talking.

The clock on the wall of Frank's office seemed to stop abruptly; there was only the present, there was only Jamie's story. It was the story I might have told Susan last night had Jamie's phone call not shattered the moment. As he spoke now, I became all of us. I was Jamie himself, confessing not to a brutal knife murder, no, but to murder nonetheless—the inexorable suffocation of his second marriage. I was Susan listening to the confession I did not make last night, but which Jamie now made *for* me. And finally, I was the victim Maureen, unable to escape the blade that came at me relentlessly in this fatal blood-spattered cage.

It was a philanderer's nightmare.

They had arranged to meet at eleven P.M. By a quarter to eleven, he was winning close to sixty dollars. He'd been betting recklessly for the past half-hour, hoping to bring his winnings down to a respectable amount that would enable him to quit without censure. But each foolish risk paid off—he drew to inside straights and filled them, he saved an ace kicker and caught the case ace, he raised with a pair of deuces and the strong hand opposite him abruptly folded. He could not seem to lose—in bed with her later he would whisper that he was lucky in cards, did that mean he was unlucky in love? He did not yet know that this was to be the unluckiest night of his life.

The poker game was his Sunday night alibi. On Wednesday afternoons, his office was closed to patients, and he went to meet her then as well. Maureen accepted his lies without question. But as he left the game on Sunday night, one of the losing players said, "Who are you rushing off to, Jamie? A girlfriend?" He'd thought the game safe until that moment. He said, "Sure, sure, a girlfriend," and waved good night—but the gratuitous comment bothered him. He was an old hand at infidelity. He'd been cheating on his first wife for half a dozen years before he met Maureen, and then he saw *her* regularly for another two years before asking for a divorce. He knew that men were worse than women when it came to gossip, and was terrified that his early departure would set them to talking about him. But he'd already left the game, he'd already taken the gamble. He could only hope to win it the way he'd won all the other reckless bets he'd made that night.

He could not understand how he had once again become involved with another woman. Catherine—he named her at last, and seemed relieved to have her name in the open, and in fact expanded upon it at once. Catherine Brenet, the wife of a Calusa surgeon, Dr. Eugene Brenet, a very good man, he said, evaluating Brenet on the basis of his medical skill and not his aptitude for cuckoldry. He'd met her at one of the charity balls, she was his dinner partner, he chatted with her, he danced with her. She was startlingly beautiful. But more than that, she was available. It was this aura of certain availability that first attracted him to her.

He was, after all, experienced at this sort of thing.

He had met this woman before; in the beginning she was only every woman he'd ever transported to clandestine assignations in countless unremembered motels. She was Goldilocks. The bitterly sarcastic name, first applied to Maureen by his former wife, now seemed to be appropriate. Goldilocks—stealing into someone else's house, testing the chairs and the porridge and especially the beds. Goldilocks, the other woman. She did not have to be blonde, though Maureen was and so was Catherine. She could just as easily have had hair as black as midnight, eyes as pale as alabaster. . . .

We were in the garden of the Leslie Harper Municipal Theater. Frank and his wife Leona, Susan and I. Statues of dwarfs surrounded us, palm fronds fluttered on the lanquid breeze. There was the scent of mimosa on the air. Leona had just introduced Agatha to the rest of us. Leona described her as a new "Harper Helper." Frank despised the term. His wife, however, was proud of her fund-raising activities for the theater, and staunchly maintained that the Harper was a very real part of Calusa's cultural scene.

Frank immediately and unequivocally said there *was* no real culture in Calusa, there was only an attempt to create an ersatz cultural *climate*. The Harper, he insisted, came close to being vanity theater. He said this within earshot of seven or eight fluttering dowagers who were themselves heavy financial supporters of what was, despite Frank's biased New York view, a good repertory theater. One of the old ladies sniffed the air as though smelling something recently deceased in the immediate vicinity. Agatha noticed this—and smiled.

I had held her hand an instant too long while being introduced, I had caught my breath too visibly at the radiance of her beauty, and now I basked too obviously in her smile. I was certain I was blushing, and I looked away at once. The warning bells chimed, signaling the end of the intermission. I looked into her pale gray eyes, she nodded almost imperceptibly, and then turned to go, black hair flailing the air. I watched as she crossed the garden to join a tall blond man whose back was to me. There was a lithe, slender catlike look about her; she took long strides over the garden stones and climbed the steps to the lobby. A sudden exciting glimpse of leg flashed in the slit of her long green gown, I held my breath and listened to the clicking chatter of her heels on the lobby terrazzo. The warning chimes sounded again. "Matthew?" Susan said, and the four of us went back into the theater. Throughout the second act I tried to locate Agatha Hemmings; the theater was small, but I could not find where she was sitting. Nor did I see her in the lobby afterward. As we walked toward where I'd parked the car, Frank pronounced the play sophomoric.

I called her on Monday morning.

Her husband's name was Gerald Hemmings, he was a building contractor. I'd learned this from Frank in a supposed rehash of our evening at the Harper together. It was good information to have. There were at least six Hemmingses in the Calusa directory, and I did not have the courage to call each and every one of them to ask if I might please speak to Agatha please. Even then, as the phone rang on the other end, I was ready to hang up if anyone other than Agatha herself answered. She answered on the fifth ring, I had been nervously counting them.

"Hello?" she said.

"Hello . . . is this Agatha Hemmings?"

"Yes?"

"Matthew Hope."

Silence.

"We met at the Harper Saturday night. Leona Summerville intro—"

"Yes, Matthew, how are you?"

"Fine. And you?"

"Fine, thank you."

Silence.

"Agatha, I . . . look, I'm about to make a complete fool of myself, I know, but . . . I'd like to see you if that's possible, for lunch if that's possible, alone, I mean, if that's possible. For lunch, I mean."

There was another silence. I was suffocating in my own air-conditioned office.

"Do we have to have lunch?" she asked.

Jamie was telling us about the first time he met Catherine alone—why had the clock stopped ticking? I did not want to hear about his sordid affair with the surgeon's promiscuous wife, I did not want this description of their first rendezvous. It was raining, he said. This was February a year ago, it was unusual for it to be raining in Calusa at this time of year. Catherine was waiting where they'd arranged. She was wearing a black raincoat and a floppy green hat that partially hid her face. He pulled the car to the curb and threw open the door, and she stepped inside at once. The black raincoat rode back to expose her leg. He put his hand on her thigh; the touch was electric. There was the aroma of wet and steamy garments in that small contained space. Daringly, he kissed her. The windshield wipers snicked at the rain. . . .

We kissed, Agatha and I, the moment we entered the motel. I had driven her seventeen miles south to the next town, but I was terrified of discovery nonetheless. When we kissed I could think only that I was a fool to be jeopardizing my marriage for an afternoon in the hay. I had convinced myself it was nothing more than that. I had not spoken to Agatha since I'd made the phone call Monday morning. This was now Thursday. I had picked her up in the parking lot behind the Calusa Bank Building at twelve sharp, and it was now a quarter to one on a Thursday in May, three weeks before my thirteenth wedding anniversary. We were kissing in a motel room, and I was scared to death. She gently took her lips from mine.

"We don't have to stay," she whispered.

"I want to stay."

"Just be sure."

"I'm sure."

She was wearing tight white slacks, a long-sleeved lavender blouse buttoned down the front. Sandals. She had rather large feet. Toenails painted a bright red. Fingernails the same color. Scarlet lipstick on her mouth, somewhat garish against the pale oval face. Her hair was the color of midnight, it shimmered with blues in the light of the single lamp. She took off her clothes without ceremony or pretense. She was dressed one moment and naked the next. Her breasts were rather smaller than I might have hoped. The black triangle of her crotch was elongated, a sexual isosceles. She came to me again and put her arms around me and kissed me on the mouth.

"I am going to love you, Matthew," she said.

Jamie was telling virtually the same story. I could have killed him for it. In this timeless chamber, soundless but for the drone of his voice, the clock silenced, time reduced to a geometrically multiplying present, I listened to him telling of his paramour, his doxie, his bimbo, his whore . . . yes, damn him, he was robbing Agatha and me of the uniqueness of our love, he was reducing *our* relationship to the level of his own, inadvertently making them *both* sound like garden-variety affairs. He now loved Catherine more than anyone in his life—*she* was his second-chance girl, he said. I remembered him saying last night, "Figure it out, how much time have I got left? I'm forty-six, what have I got left, another thirty years?" Forty-six was his age now, his age today, his age last night when he said, "This was my second chance, supposed to be my second chance." What he'd meant was his *second* second chance, two to the second power, *not* Maureen, but the round-heels surgeon's wife he'd been in bed with while Maureen was being slaughtered.

I felt suddenly faint.

If he did not stop talking I would collapse. He was proclaiming his love for Catherine, telling how together last night they'd talked about their respective mates—he used that word, *mates,* as though he were a sailor or perhaps an Englishman in a pub, *mates;* I had never heard anyone before, man or woman, referring to a marital partner as a mate. But Maureen was most certainly his mate, just as Dr. Eugene Brenet was Catherine's mate. And Susan was mine, and a man I had never met was Agatha's. A man named Gerald Hemmings, whom she would leave the moment I told my wife, my mate, that I was in love with another woman.

Jamie and his mistress had made the same decision, they made it last night in the place they rented on Whisper Key—this had, after all, been going on for more than a year now, they had advanced well beyond the motel stage, they could afford to rent a small cottage on the beach where they could make love. They promised to tell their respective mates soon, they obviously couldn't go on this way. *Soon, my darling, soon*—he was describing their passionate farewell now, Catherine in his arms, kissing her face, her throat, I did not want to listen. Was this why I was ready to end my own marriage? So that seven years from now I could begin another affair with yet another woman, the Maureens and Catherines and Agathas of this world multiplying into an endless sorority of fornicating surgeons' wives or court stenographers, cocktail waitresses or kindergarten teachers, one and all the same akimbo, each and all named Goldilocks?

He was on Jacaranda Drive now, he was pulling his car into the garage. The lights were on, this wasn't strange, Maureen usually left them on when he was out playing poker. He cut the ignition and came around to the side door of the house, unlocked it. He was hoping she would be asleep. She sometimes waited up for him, but he hoped she hadn't done that now. He was flushed with excitement, but this was not the time to tell her about his plans, not yet, he did not want her forcing his hand by asking unanswerable questions.

He snapped on the bedroom lights.

He saw the blood-spattered walls first.

He almost backed out of the room. He thought someone had, he thought his daughters, he thought, he did not know it was blood at first, he thought someone had soiled the walls. The blood smears were not the color of the bright red stripe that follows a surgeon's scalpel and wells up into the incision, they were not the black-red of blood in a syringe or a bottle, they were almost brown. He thought at first—these were all instantaneous ideas that flashed into his mind with stopwatch frequency—he thought someone had smeared feces on the walls.

The closet door was open, and he saw her hand protruding from inside the closet, palm upward. He moved to the closet door. He stopped. He looked down at the hand. He said, "Oh, my God," and opened the door. He realized at once that she must have run into the closet to hide, her final refuge from whoever had slashed her nightgown to flowing tatters of nylon, her body to ribbons of flesh. There was a rosette on the bodice of the gown, it registered as a small pink eye against the blood-drenched pink of the gown itself. Her face was almost unrecognizable. There were deep gashes across her breasts, and her throat had been cut from one ear to the other so that there was a wide, grinning bloody mouth below her own mouth gaping at the ceiling. He knelt quickly beside her and closed her eyes, thinking absurdly that she should not witness this horror.

And then he remembered the children.

He got to his feet. He stumbled to the door and down the corridor to their room, thinking, praying they were asleep, hoping the sounds of her struggle had not awakened the children, had not revealed to the intruder that there were two young girls in this house besides the woman he'd already killed.

He almost tripped over Emily in the doorway to the bedroom.

He backed away, he backed away.

He screamed—

The telephone shrilled into the sudden stillness of Frank's office. He picked it up immediately.

"Hello?" he said. "Yes, Cynthia." He looked at me. "For you, Matt."

It was Betty Purchase, Jamie's former wife, telling me she'd just been visited by a Detective Ehrenberg of the Calusa Police Department, and asking if I could come to her house at once.

6

THE LAST time I'd spoken to Betty was in January, when I'd threatened her with a partition sale, and she'd told me to go ahead and sue, Charlie. She was rather more cordial now as she ushered me into the huge house she had once shared with Jamie. I knew her, of course, I had run into her at cocktail parties here and there around town; it was impossible to live in a place like Calusa without meeting everyone sooner or later. She was wearing a gray tailored pants suit, a brandy-colored blouse showing in the V of the jacket opening. Her black hair was cropped close to her head in a shingle bob. Her eyes were a deep brown. She was not an unattractive woman, but there was a tight, pinched look to her face, and it communicated an anger that seemed volatile and dangerous. She walked with a stiff, unwomanly gait—I recalled abruptly that Jamie had described her as frigid for the first thirteen years of their marriage. On the deck, she offered me a chair, and then took a chair opposite me. Beyond, the ocean crashed in against a mile-long stretch of white sand beach. The house and the grounds had been part of the divorce settlement. The rest, according to Jamie, had been two hundred thousand dollars in cash, and thirty thousand a year in alimony.

She offered me a drink. I declined; it was still only eleven-thirty in the morning. She asked if I would care for some coffee. Some iced tea? Again, I declined. Then, without preamble, she said, "I want to know what Jamie told the police."

"About what?"

"About me."

"Only that you were once married."

"Then why did they come here asking questions? Did Jamie tell them I might have had something to do with the murders?"

"No, he did not."

"I don't believe you."

"You should have expected the police," I said. "A visit to a former wife would seem routine in a case—"

"No, it wasn't routine, don't tell me it was *routine*," she said sharply, and rose abruptly and began pacing.

"Betty," I said, "on the phone, you told me you wanted to talk to Jamie's attorney. Okay. I'm here. I've already told you that Jamie didn't even *hint*—"

"Then why do they think I might have done it?"

"Did they say they thought so?"

"They wanted to know where I was last night."

"What'd you tell them?"

"I told them I was here."

"Then what are you worried about?"

"They wanted to know if anyone was with me. I told them no one was with me, I was here alone watching television. I'm a woman without a husband, I'm forty-two years old, where the hell did they *think* I'd be on a Sunday night?"

"Betty, I still don't understand why—"

"Don't you? They wanted to know what television shows I'd been watching, whether I'd made any phone calls or received any, what time I went to bed. What does that sound like to you?"

"Routine questioning. If you'd in fact talked to anyone on the phone—"

"I didn't talk to a goddamn soul all night," she said. "My phone doesn't ring too often these days." The eyes were tighter now, the mouth thin. "I'm a woman alone in a town full of divorcées and widows. When a man can find himself a twenty-year-old in a bar or on a beach, he's not too inclined . . ."

"What I'm saying—"

"What you're saying is that a telephone call would have substantiated my alibi, isn't that what you're saying?"

"You used the word, Betty, not me."

"I don't *need* an alibi, I didn't kill that bitch."

"I'm sure you told that to the police."

"Yes, I told them. But I saw them ringing doorbells after they left here. One of my neighbors phoned later to say they'd asked her whether she'd seen any lights on in the house last night, whether the car was in the garage—"

"*Were* there any lights on?"

"Only in the television den, on the beach side. No one on the street side could have seen them. And the garage door was closed, none of my neighbors would have had any way of knowing whether I was home or not."

"But you were home. You just told me . . ."

"Yes, I was home."

"Then what are you worried about, Betty?"

"I don't want to get involved in this. I've got a reputation to protect in this town, it isn't easy for a woman alone. My life is difficult enough as it is, Jamie robbed me of my dignity, and my pride, and now he's . . . with his, with his big mouth he's suggesting—"

"He's suggesting no such thing. I was with him during the police interrogation. Not once did he cast the slightest . . . look, Betty, what the hell do you want?"

"I'll tell you what I *don't* want. I don't want anyone coming around here again asking me questions about where I was, treating me like a common criminal, just because Jamie—"

"Jamie said nothing to—"

"You give him a message for me, okay? You tell him that if I hear he's so much as breathed a word to anyone—and I mean *anyone*—about a possible connection between me and those murders, I'll sue him for slander before he can bat an eyelash. You go tell him that."

"Is that why you asked me to come here?"

"Yes. You're his attorney. He should be warned. I don't

want anyone snooping into my private life. He embarrassed me enough when he . . . when he *flaunted* his goddamn affairs to the whole town, started living with Goldilocks even before we'd reached a settlement, eighteen *months,* the son of a bitch, living with her in that little love nest on Stone Crab. You tell him what I said, Matt. You warn him—"

"I'll warn him, but I hardly think a warning is necessary."

"Tell him what I said."

"I will."

"And tell him something else."

Her back was to the ocean, the sun hung almost at its zenith, illuminating the sand and the water with a harsh flat glare. Her eyes met mine.

"Tell him I'm glad they're dead."

"I don't think you want me to tell him that, Betty."

"Tell him," she said. "Tell the rotten bastard."

I wasn't surprised that Ehrenberg had been to see her. I knew very little about the man as yet, but I suspected he would take nothing for granted in this case—not Jamie's alibi, *nor* the whereabouts of his former wife on the night of the murders. I felt certain that it would only be a matter of time before he learned all about Jamie's hurried departure from the poker game and his subsequent assignation with Catherine Brenet. I felt certain, too, that he would not accept Betty's alibi on her word alone. If no one had seen lights in the house, if no one could say positively that Betty had indeed been home last night, then she could have been anywhere. And anywhere might have been Jacaranda Drive, where Maureen and the children were being killed.

I thought about this all the way back to the office. The murders had been committed in apparent rage, and if there was one thing Betty Purchase had in abundance, it was anger. I wondered if I should call Ehrenberg to repeat what she'd said just before I'd left the house—*"Tell him I'm glad they're dead."* I didn't have to call him. When I got to the office, Cynthia told me he himself had phoned not five minutes earlier to report that Jamie's son Michael had confessed to the murders.

In Calusa, the police station is officially called the Public Safety Building, and these words are lettered in white on the low wall outside. Less conspicuously lettered to the right on the brown metal entrance doors, and partially obscured by Pittosporum bushes, are the words Police Department. The building is constructed of varying shades of tan brick and its architecturally severe face is broken only by narrow windows resembling rifle slits in an armory wall. This is not unusual for Calusa, where the summer months are torrid and large windows produce only heat and glare. I entered the building, and walked directly to what was obviously a reception desk. One of the girls there told me I could find Detective Ehrenberg and Dr. Purchase on the third floor, and then buzzed Ehrenberg to let him know I was on the way. He and Jamie were waiting for me when I stepped off the elevator into the corridor. Ehrenberg looked sympathetic and grave, and he said at once, "I've already told Dr. Purchase how sorry I am about this."

"I'd like to talk to Michael," I said. "*Alone*, Jamie."

"That's usually best," Ehrenberg said, and nodded reassuringly. I did not for a moment doubt that the arrest of twenty-year-old Michael Purchase had upset him. He seemed to be a man who could not easily hide his feelings or pretend to feelings that weren't genuine. He was disturbed by the turn of the events, and it showed on his face and in the slump of his shoulders. His hands were in his pockets. He seemed almost ashamed of the fact that we were here on a bright sunny afternoon to examine the bloody deeds of a midnight just passed.

"All right," Jamie said, "but, please, I want to see him before—"

"You can talk to him before we question him," Ehrenberg said. "But then it'll have to be just his attorney present, if he wants one."

"I may have to call in a criminal lawyer," I said.

"If that's what the boy wants, fine."

"Have you talked to him yet?"

"Why, no, sir," Ehrenberg said. He looked suddenly injured.

"You said he's confessed to the murders . . ."

"Yes, but that was to the arresting officer. That was still a field investigation, the officer wasn't required to read him *Miranda-Escobedo*. We advised him of his rights the minute he was in custody here at this facility. He said he wanted us to call his father, and we finally reached Dr. Purchase at your office."

"All right," I said, "let me talk to him, please."

He had walked us into a large reception area dominated by an orange letter-elevator that rose like an oversize periscope from the floor diagonally opposite the entrance doors. There was a desk against the paneled wall facing us, and a girl sat behind it, typing furiously. The clock on the wall above her head read twelve-fifteen.

"He's in the captain's office," Ehrenberg said. "If you'll have a seat on the bench here, Dr. Purchase, I'll find somebody to bring you a cup of coffee." He indicated the bench, and then led me past an American flag in a floor stand, to where another pair of doors stood at right angles to each other in a small alcove. He opened the door on our left, and I went into the room. The door clicked shut behind me.

At first I thought the office was empty. There was a desk on the wall opposite, a green leatherette swivel chair behind it. On the paneled wall above the desk, several framed diplomas. Bookshelves behind the desk, a hookah pipe on the top shelf. Framed photos of women I guessed were the captain's wife and daughters. From the corner of my eye, I saw Michael Purchase sitting in a chair to the right of the door, and walked to him at once.

His elbows were resting on his thighs, his hands were clenched forward of his knees, his head was bent, almost level with the polished top of the captain's desk. He did not look up as I approached. His eyes remained focused instead on the desk top, where half a dozen Polaroid pictures of a black girl were spread in a row that resembled a lineup of sextuplets. Michael was wearing blood-stained blue jeans and a blood-stained white T-shirt. His sandals were caked with what seemed to be a mixture of dried blood and sand. There was sand in his matted black hair, blood on his cheek, blood caked in the curve of his ear.

"Michael," I said.

He looked up at me, brown eyes wide in his narrow face, and nodded bleakly, and then went back to studying the pictures of the black girl. I could not believe he was really seeing them. I felt only that he chose not to meet my eyes.

"I have some questions for you, Michael."

He nodded again.

"Did you kill Maureen and your sisters?"

He nodded.

"Michael, I want you to speak, please. I want you to answer yes or no. Did you kill Maureen?"

"Yes," he said. His voice was hoarse. He cleared his throat. "Yes," he said again.

"And the girls?"

"Yes."

"Who'd you tell this to?"

"The cop."

"Which cop?"

"The one who arrested me."

"Where was this?"

"Sabal Beach."

"What time?"

"About ten? I'm not sure. I haven't got a watch."

"Is he the only one you told it to?"

"Yes."

"Michael," I said, "I want to get a criminal lawyer for you. I'm not equipped to handle something like this myself, I want to call in someone who is. The best criminal lawyer in town is probably Benny Freid, I want to call him, I want to get him in here immediately."

"No," Michael said, and shook his head.

"I'm advising you as your attorney—"

"You're not my attorney, nobody asked for you. I don't

need you, and I don't need a criminal lawyer, either. I killed them."

"In this state, the penalty for first-degree murder is—"

"Fine, let them—"

"The electric chair."

"Fine."

"Michael, they're going to start questioning you in just a little while. I want to call Benny before then. He's a friend of mine, I feel reasonably sure he'll—"

"I don't want him. Don't call him because I don't want him."

"What exactly did you say to the patrolman who arrested you?"

"I don't remember."

"Did you say you'd killed somebody?"

"Yes."

"Did you say *who* you'd killed? Did you say you'd killed Maureen Purchase and Emily Purchase and Eve Purchase?"

"No, I didn't say that."

"What *did* you say exactly, can you remember?"

"I said I did it."

"Did what?"

"Killed them."

"Were those your exact words? Did you say 'I did it, I killed them'?"

"What *difference* does it make?" he shouted, and rose suddenly. "I did it, I did it, what more do you want?"

"I want to know what you told that patrolman."

"He came on me in the woods, okay? I was sleeping in the woods."

"What woods?"

"Off Sabal Shores. The pine forest going down to the beach. North Sabal."

"Near your father's house?"

"Yes. You walk to the end of Jacaranda, and then you climb over the chain across the driveway on West Lane, and you're in the pine forest. I was sleeping there when he found me."

"He woke you up?"

"Yes."

"And you say this was about ten o'clock?"

"I told you I don't have a watch, I don't know what time it was."

"All right, he woke you up. What'd he say?"

"He wanted to know what I was doing there. I told him I was sleeping."

"Then what?"

"He asked me did I have any identification. I showed him my driver's license, and he looked at the picture on it —I had a beard when I took the picture, he made some comment about it, I forget what he said . . . look, what's the *sense* of this, would you please tell me? Let's get it *over* with, for Christ's sake!"

"Over with? Michael, they're going to charge you with murder!"

"I *know* what they're going to charge me with, what do you *think* they're going to charge me with?"

"Tell me what happened with the patrolman."

"Why?"

"Because I want to know what you said to him. I want to know what gave him the idea you'd killed Maureen and—"

"The *idea?*" Michael said, and rolled his eyes, and shook his head in disbelief. "It's not an *idea,* it's a *fact.* I *did* kill them. Can't you understand that? I killed them, and I want to confess to the crime and get it over with. That's what *I* want to do, and all *you* want to do is find out what I told the goddamn patrolman. That's what I told him. That I killed them. That's what I'm telling you. I killed them."

"Were those your exact words?"

"Man, you never *quit,* do you?" Michael said, and let out his breath in exasperation. "I showed him the license, right? He looked at the beard in the picture, right? He said something about did I shave off the beard, and I said Yeah, and then he said Michael Purchase, is that your name? and I said Yeah, that's my name. He looked at me and he said Are you any relation to Dr. James Purchase? and I said Yes, I'm his son. Then he said How long've you been here in these woods, Michael? and I said I couldn't remember, I'd just gone in there and I guess I'd fallen asleep. So he asked me when I went in there and I guessed it was last night sometime, and he said *When* last night? I told him I didn't remember. He said Where'd you get that blood on your clothes, Michael? I looked at him, he . . . he was looking me right in the eye, he said again Where'd you get that blood on your clothes, Michael? And I just nodded and said Okay, I did it."

"Then what?"

"He had a walkie-talkie on his belt, he switched it on and called for somebody to get down there right away, said he had the killer."

"Did he use that word?"

"Which word? Killer?"

"Yes."

"I don't know. He either said killer or murderer, I don't know."

"All right, Michael, now listen to me. If you don't want me to call in a lawyer who can help you more than I can, then you've got to at least listen to me and do what I ask you to do. Ehrenberg's going to question you about last night. I want you to remain silent, Michael. That's your privilege. They've already read your rights to you once, and I'm sure they'll read them again before they start questioning you, and they'll tell you it's your privilege to remain silent, and that's what I want you to do. I don't want you to say another word about any of this. Not another word. Have you got that?"

"I've got it," he said, "but it's not what I want to do."

"Michael . . ."

"I want to tell them."

Jamie was waiting for me when I came out of the captain's office. I told him essentially what his son had said, and he nodded and then asked Ehrenberg if it was all right for him to talk to Michael now. Ehrenberg told him to go on in. As soon as the door closed behind him, I said, "Mr. Ehrenberg, the boy's about to make a statement against my advice. There's nothing I can do about it, but I want to sit in on the questioning anyway."

"That's fine with me," Ehrenberg said. "Few things I

wanted to discuss with you while the father's in there with him. First off, I checked with some of those people who were at the poker game last night, and it seems the doctor *wasn't* losing when he left, way he told it to me, but instead was winning something like sixty, seventy dollars. Told the other players he was tired and wanted to go home, get some sleep. Now that doesn't sound like a man who later spent an hour and a half drinking at The Innside Out. I don't know *where* he went when he left that poker game, but I do know he was lying about being a loser, and my guess is he was lying about The Innside Out, too.

"I haven't yet been able to reach the bartender who was on duty last night, but I spoke to the owners this morning, nice couple, they told me the bar was relatively quiet last night, maybe a half-dozen people in there around the time Dr. Purchase says he was there. So chances are if I go around with a picture of him, or even run a lineup for the bartender or the fellow they've got entertaining there, one or the other'll recognize him if he was *really* there. Meanwhile, I'm wondering why he lied to me. I guess you asked him did he have anything to do with those murders?"

"I asked him."

"And I'm assuming he told you the same thing he told me, that he didn't commit those murders."

"That's what he told me."

"That's what the wife said, too, the former wife. I went to see her this morning, she claims she was home all night last night. Only trouble is, none of the neighbors are able to say for sure whether she was or not. Oh yes, she can reel off the television shows she watched, but anybody could've got those from the *TV Guide*. I'm telling you all this, Mr. Hope, because I don't know what's going on with the boy saying right off he did it. I'll be questioning him in just a little bit now, soon as his father's done in there, but in the meantime it looks like I've got a man who was maybe lying about where he actually was at the time of the murders, and a woman who says she was home when for all I know she was maybe—"

"You little son of a bitch."

The voice was Jamie's, the words came from behind the closed door to the captain's office. A pained look came onto Ehrenberg's face as he turned and began walking heavily toward the door, as though Jamie's outburst was not entirely unexpected, but was nonetheless an additional problem that had to be dealt with. As he approached the door, Jamie shouted, "I'll kill you!" and Ehrenberg responded to the threat instinctively and immediately. He seemed almost about to thrust his massive shoulder against the door in imitation of movie cops breaking into a suspect apartment. He grabbed the knob and did indeed use his shoulder, but only as a forceless battering ram, opening the door and throwing it wide, and then releasing the knob and rushing into the room, directly to where Jamie and Michael were struggling in front of the captain's desk.

Jamie's hands were on his son's throat. His face was ashen, his mouth skinned back over his teeth, his eyes red with rage. Michael danced a jig at the ends of his father's arms, stepping again and again onto the photographs of the black girl that had earlier been on the captain's desk and were now strewn on the floor. His face was flushed, he was choking under tightening pressure of his father's fingers. Ehrenberg clamped his left hand onto Jamie's shoulder and spun him back and away from his son. I thought for certain he was going to smash his fist into Jamie's face. It seemed the logical one-two action, spin the man around with your left hand, hit him with your right. But instead of hitting him, Ehrenberg reached out with his right hand to grab hold of the lapels of Jamie's leisure suit, his fist twisting into the material. Effortlessly, he pushed him back against the paneled wall. Very calmly he said, "Now let's just relax, doctor."

"I'll kill him," Jamie said.

"No, you're not going to kill anybody," Ehrenberg said.

"*Kill* the bastard," Jamie said.

Across the room, Michael was still gasping for breath. "You okay?" Ehrenberg asked, and Michael nodded. "Then I'd like to talk to you now, if that's all right with you."

"Yes," Michael said. "Okay."

"You *monster,*" his father said.

7

THE INTERVIEW room was a five-by-eight rectangle with a small table and three armless chairs in it. There was a mirror, on the wall facing Michael. I suspected it was a two-way mirror, and asked Ehrenberg if it was. He readily admitted that it was, and then assured me that no photographs were being taken and that none would be taken until Michael was officially charged with a crime. He said this while fiddling with the tape recorder he'd carried from the squad room into the interview room. I knew that "interview" was a euphemism for "interrogation," but I made no comment. I was fully cognizant of the fact that Michael Purchase was determined to make a statement to the police, and that if I said anything or did anything to annoy him he would simply ask me to leave. Moreover, I was thoroughly convinced that Ehrenberg had done nothing to jeopardize Michael's constitutional rights, nor would he do so at any time during the interview, or interrogation, or whatever he chose to call it. I had the feeling he preferred the word "interview." I had the feeling that everything about police work, and especially about this case, troubled him. I visualized him as an antiques dealer in some New England town. I visualized him as a man running a nursery someplace, selling potted hyacinths or gloxinias. The room was air-conditioned, but Ehrenberg was perspiring as he spoke a few test words into the recorder, played them back, and reset the machine for taping.

Into the microphone he said, "This will be a recording of the questions put to Michael Purchase and of his responses thereto made this first day of March at . . ." He looked at his watch. ". . . twelve twenty-seven P.M. in the Public Safety Building of the Calusa Police Department, Calusa, Florida. Questioning Mr. Purchase was Detective George Ehrenberg of the Calusa Police Department. Also present was Mr. Matthew Hope of the law firm of Summerville & Hope, Carey Avenue, Calusa, attorney for Mr. Purchase."

He hesitated, looked briefly at Michael and me, as if to make certain he'd mentioned all the people sitting at the table, and then said, "I know you've previously been informed of your rights, Mr. Purchase, but I'd like to go over them again, for the record. In keeping with the Supreme Court decision in *Miranda* vs. *Arizona,* we are not permitted to ask you any questions until you are warned of your right to counsel and your privilege against self-incrimination. So first, you have the right to remain silent. Do you understand that?"

"Yes, I do," Michael said.

He went through the rest of the obligatory recitation, making certain that Michael understood all of his rights, ascertaining that Michael was willing to have me present as his attorney, and then asking him his full name, soliciting from Michael the information that he was living at present on a boat called *The Broadhorn,* which was docked at Pirate's Cove, and that a girl named Lisa Schellmann . . .

"Would you spell that, please?" Ehrenberg said.

"S-C-H-E-L-L-M-A-N-N."

. . . was living with him, had been living with him for the past two months, in fact. He asked Michael how old he was, asked if Dr. James Purchase was his father, asked if Maureen was his stepmother and Emily and Eve his half sisters, and then took a deep breath and said, "Will you tell me, please, as best you can recall, what took place on the night of February twenty-ninth, that would have been last night, Sunday the twenty-ninth of February."

"Where do you want me to begin?" Michael asked.

"Were you in the vicinity of Jacaranda Drive on Sabal Shores at any time last night?"

"I was, sir, yes, sir."

"Where on Jacaranda?"

"At my father's house."

"At the home of Dr. James Purchase?"

"Yes, sir, my father."

"Why did you go there?"

"To see him."

"To see your father? Could you speak up, please? And into the mike, please."

"Yes, sir, I'm sorry."

"Why did you want to see your father?"

"I needed some money. For a repair on the boat."

"What sort of repair?"

"She's leaking drive oil into the engine pan."

"And you went there to talk to your father about it."

"Yeah, to ask him if I could borrow some money to have it fixed. It's going to cost six hundred dollars."

"Did you go to his house directly from the boat?"

"Yes, sir."

"Did you drive from Pirate's Cove to Sabal Shores?"

"No, I don't have a car. I got a hitch from some people coming out of the restaurant there. They dropped me off on the corner of Jacaranda."

"What time was this?"

"Was what? When I got to Jacaranda?"

"Yes."

"About a quarter to twelve, I guess. I don't have a watch."

"Did you walk up Jacaranda directly to the house?"

"Yes, directly to the house."

"Were there lights on when you got there?"

"Yes."

"Outside lights? Inside lights?"

"Both."

"What did you do when you got to the house?"

"I went to the front door and rang the bell."

"Did your father answer the doorbell?"

"No. Maureen did."

"What did she say?"

"She seemed . . . ah . . . she was surprised to see me. It was close to midnight, I guess it was late to be paying a visit."

"Did she say anything about it being late?"

"No, no."

"What did she say?"

"She just . . . ah . . . said my father wasn't home."

"Did she say *where* he was?"

"No. Just that he wasn't home."

"Do you know where he was last night, Mr. Purchase?"

"No, sir, I do not."

"When you went to the house, did you know he wouldn't be home?"

"Well . . . no. I expected him to be there."

"You didn't know Sunday night was his poker night."

"No, I thought he'd be home. I was going there to see him."

"But now that I remind you of it, do you recall that your father customarily plays poker every other Sunday?"

"Yes, I guess I know that."

I wanted to stop the questioning then and there, but I hesitated. Ehrenberg wasn't trying to trick Michael, it wasn't that, nor was he putting words in his mouth. His job was to get the facts, and he was simply doing his job. But he knew that once this session was finished, the police would have to charge Michael, and what Michael said in the next little while would largely determine the nature of the charge. I had not looked at the state's criminal statutes since the time I'd been studying for the Florida bar exams, but I knew well enough that to charge Michael with first degree murder, there had to be a reasonable assumption of "premeditated design." Ehrenberg was trying to find out whether or not Michael went to that house with the express purpose of killing Maureen and the two girls. He had just admitted that he now remembered his father played poker every other Sunday night. I knew what Ehrenberg's next question would be, and I wanted to stop it before he asked it. But I was afraid Michael would then request that I be kicked summarily out of the room. My situation was a delicate one. I waited, hoping Ehrenberg wouldn't ask the anticipated question. He asked it.

"Mr. Purchase, did you in fact *know* your father wouldn't be home last night when you went—"

"Michael," I said, "as your attorney, I think I should advise you to stop answering any more questions at this point. Mr. Ehrenberg, I think you can realize the position—"

"I want to answer the questions," Michael said.

"You've been warned that anything you say here can be used as evidence against you. The purpose of an attorney—"

"I *want* to," Michael said, and then answered the question in a way that still left the matter of premeditation unresolved. "I really didn't know where he'd be," he said. "I didn't know whether he'd be at the house or not. That's the truth."

"But when you got there—"

"He wasn't there."

"This was at a quarter to twelve?"

"Around then."

"What time would it have been *exactly?*"

Ehrenberg was going after facts again. An autopsy was mandatory in a murder case, that much I knew. If he did not already have the information in his possession, Ehrenberg would soon have from the coroner an approximate time of death. If the coroner said Maureen and the girls had been killed sometime between eleven and midnight, for example, and Michael now stated he'd got there at . . .

"It would have been about a quarter to twelve, maybe a little later," he said. "I told you, I don't have a watch."

"So at a quarter to twelve, you rang the doorbell—"

"Yes."

"And your stepmother answered it."

"Maureen answered it, yes, sir."

"What was she wearing?"

"A nightgown."

"Just a nightgown?"

"Yes . . . ah . . . a pink nightgown."

"She opened the door wearing just the nightgown."

"Yes."

"A long nightgown or a short nightgown?"

"Long."

"Did it have sleeves?"

"No, no sleeves."

"Can you tell me anything else about the nightgown?"

"I think . . . yes, there was a sort of a little rosebud thing here at the . . . where the . . . the neck, this part of the gown."

"You're indicating an area . . . oh, midway on your chest."

"Yes."

"Where a woman's breasts would be."

"Yes."

"And you say there was . . . a *rosebud,* did you call it?"

"I don't know what it's called, it's a little sort of . . . the fabric is gathered, it looks like a flower."

"Would you mean a rosette?"

"Yes, that's right, a rosette."

"What color was the rosette?"

"Pink, same as the gown."

"What else was your stepmother wearing?"

"That's all, I think."

"Slippers?"

"No."

"Jewelry?"

"A wedding band."

"Anything in her hair?"

"No."

He had just described exactly what Maureen was wearing. I'd heard this same description from Jamie two hours earlier, when he was telling us about walking into that bedroom and finding his wife in the closet. Even the rosette, Michael had just described even the goddamn rosette. I had to make another try. This time, I directed my plea to Ehrenberg.

"Mr. Ehrenberg," I said, "on behalf of my client, I'd like to protest strongly this continuing interrogation after I've advised him to—"

"Listen," Michael said, his voice rising, "you just shut the fuck up, okay?"

"Everything you say is being taped—"

"I know it is."

"And can be used later as—"

"Damn it, will you please let me—"

"Mr. Ehrenberg," I said, "can you stop the tape a minute?"

Ehrenberg immediately pushed the STOP button.

The room went silent.

"Michael," I said, "I'm going to ask you just one question. If you answer yes to it, I'll keep still for the rest of this interview, you can say whatever you like, I won't interrupt, I won't try to stop you. But if you say no—"

"What's the question?"

"Do you want to go to the electric chair?"

"Yes."

Ehrenberg visibly flinched. I don't think he was expecting Michael's affirmative reply; I know I wasn't.

"So can we please get on with it?" Michael said.

Ehrenberg looked at me, waiting for my permission to continue. I said nothing. He nodded helplessly and pressed the RECORD button. His voice was softer when he began questioning Michael again. "Would you tell me what happened next, please?" he said.

"Maureen told me my father wasn't home, and ah . . . asked me if I wanted to come in."

"Did you go in?"

"Yes, sir."

"Through the front door?"

"Yes."

"Where did you go? What part of the house?"

"Well . . . ah . . . first we went into the kitchen."

"Yes, go on."

"We sat down in the kitchen."

"Yes."

"There's a table there in the kitchen."

"Go on."

"And while we were sitting there . . . it's hard for me to remember all this."

"I know it is. But while you were sitting at the kitchen table . . ."

"I guess I saw the knives."

"What knives?"

"There's a rack on the wall. In the kitchen. It's a magnetic rack, there're four or five knives on it. You know, different kinds of knives."

"What happened when you saw this rack with the knives on it?"

"I guess I . . . ah . . . got up and grabbed one of the knives from the rack."

"Which knife?"

"It had to be one of the big knives."

"Can you describe the knife more particularly?'"

"No, I don't really remember what it looked like. One of the big ones on the rack. I just . . . I just reached up and grabbed the . . . nearest knife."

"But you don't remember *which* knife it was."

"I know it was one of the big ones."

"How many big ones were there on the rack?"

"I don't know."

"But you reached for one of them."

"Yes."

"Reached *how?* Can you show me where the knife rack was in relationship to the table here in this room?"

"Yes, it was . . . it would have been to the right. I got up, and I walked to the right, and I took the knife off the rack."

"What did Maureen say when she saw you doing this?"

"Nothing. I don't remember."

"What were you talking about before you reached for the knife?"

"I don't remember."

"Well, was it a pleasant conversation?"

"I don't remember."

"Would you remember why you got up and reached for the knife?"

"I just got up and grabbed it from the rack."

"What did you do then?"

"I stabbed her."

"Were you still in the kitchen when you stabbed her?"

"Yes. Well, no, actually, we were . . . it was in the bedroom."

"How did you get to the bedroom?"

"I don't remember. I guess she ran in there."
"And you followed her?"
"Yes."
"With the knife?"
"Yes."
"In which hand were you holding the knife?"
"My right hand."
"Are you right-handed?"
"Yes."
"Were you holding the knife in your right hand when you stabbed her?"
"Yes."
"Did she scream?"
"Her mouth."
"What about her mouth?"
"It was open."
"She was screaming, is that it?"
"No."
"But her mouth was open?"
"Yes."
"Did she say anything to you?"
"No."
"Where was she when you stabbed her?"
"On the . . . near the . . . she was . . . in the . . . in the . . . I didn't see her at first, she was . . . there was . . ."
"All right, Mr. Purchase, calm down now. Calm down, please."
"Yes, I'm sorry."
"Would you like a glass of water?"
"No, thank you."
"Just try to . . ."
"Yes."
"Compose yourself."
"Yes."
"When you're ready to continue—"
"I'm ready now."
"Just tell me again what happened in the bedroom."
"I stabbed her."
"Where was she?"
"In the closet."
"What was she doing in the closet?"

"I didn't see her at first. I was looking."

"But you didn't see her."

"Not at first."

"And when you did see her . . . ?"

"Yes."

"What happened after you saw her?"

"I . . . stabbed her."

"How many times did you stab her?"

"I don't remember."

"Were you angry?"

"Sad."

"Why were you sad?"

"She was dead."

"You were sad that you'd killed her?"

"It was true."

"What was true?"

"She was dead."

"Had you thought it *wasn't* true?"

"I was wishing . . . I kept wishing it was a mistake."

"I don't understand. You kept wishing *what* was a mistake?"

"That she was dead."

"When did you realize it *wasn't* a mistake?"

"Well, I saw her . . . she . . . when I saw her on the floor . . . with . . . the gown all torn . . . all slashed . . . and . . . her . . . her throat cut, I . . . I knew she was dead, I knew it was true, and I . . . I took her in my arms. I held her, I rocked her . . ."

"Why did you do that?"

"I was crying."

"Was this after you realized she was dead?"

"Yes, after I realized."

"Is that how you got the blood on your clothes?"

"Yes."

"When you held your stepmother in your arms?"

"Yes. And my sister Emily. I held Emily in my arms, too."

"Did you also embrace Eve?"

"No, Eve was . . . under the covers. I . . . just Emily. I just held Emily."

"When was this?"

"I . . . I lifted her . . . she was on the floor inside the door."

"Are we talking about Emily now?"

"Yes, Emily."

"What was *she* wearing?"

"A short nightgown and . . . panties."

"What color was the nightgown?"

"A pale blue."

"Did it have sleeves?"

"No."

"What color were the panties?"

"I don't know."

"What was Eve wearing?"

"I don't know. She was under the covers."

"But Emily wasn't in bed?"

"No."

"When did you go into the girls' room?"

"Afterward."

"After what?"

"After Maureen."

"Why did you go into the girl's room?"

"Maureen was dead, I wanted to . . ."

"Yes?"

"I went in to see the girls."

"Were you still carrying the knife?"

"What?"

"The knife. Was it—"

"Yes."

"Still in your hand?"

"Yes."

"You still had the knife in your hand."

"Yes, I . . . still had it."

"So you went into the girls' room with the knife in your hand."

"Yes."

"What did you do then?"

"I stabbed the girls, too."

"Which of the girls did you stab first?"

"Emily. She was just inside the door."

"She was out of bed, and was standing just inside the door, is that it?"

"She was . . . yes. Yes, that's it."

"Did you say anything to her?"

"No."

"How many times did you stab her?"

"A lot. It had to be a lot."

"Did she scream?"

"I don't remember."

"What did you do then?"

"I went to the bed where Eve was. Against the wall. And I . . . ah . . . I stabbed her, too."

"Through the covers?"

"Through the covers."

"Then what did you do?"

"I left the house."

"You said you embraced your sister—"

"What?"

"Emily. You said you embraced—"

"Yes, that must have . . . that was . . . I guess after I stabbed Eve, I . . . on the way out of the room, I . . . Emily was on the floor just inside the door, I . . . held her, too, I . . . knelt down beside her and just . . . held her in my arms, and I suppose I was crying, I suppose I was still crying. Because it was all so goddamn sad, it was all so sad."

"What did you do then? After you embraced Emily."

"I put her gently . . . I lowered her gently to the . . . the floor again, and I left the house."

"Through the front door?"

"No."

"You did not leave the way you came in?"

"No."

"Why not?"

"I had blood on my clothes."

"How did you leave?"

"Through the door at the side of the house. I locked it behind me."

"How?"

"I twisted the button on the doorknob."

"All right, you went out through the side door and then where did you go? Can you describe your route?"

"I began walking west toward the beach."

"Were you still carrying the knife?"

"I . . . don't remember."

"Where *is* that knife, can you tell me?"

"I don't know."

"You don't know what happened to the knife?"

"No."

"Did you leave it in the house?"

"I don't remember."

"Or throw it away someplace on the grounds?"

"I don't remember."

"Did you walk toward the bayou when you came out of the house?"

"No."

"You didn't go anywhere near the bayou?"

"No."

"So you couldn't have thrown the knife in the water there at the back of the house."

"I don't remember."

"But you *do* remember that you didn't go toward the bayou?"

"That's right."

"You left the house—"

"Yes. And came around the side of it, and began walking west on Jacaranda, toward the beach."

"Did you still have the knife in your hand?"

"I guess so."

"What did you do then?"

"There's this property that belongs . . . it's an access road to the beach, it belongs to the people who live in the development, a private access road. There's a chain across the entrance to it, I climbed over the chain, and walked down through the pine forest—"

"Still carrying the knife?"

"I don't remember."

"Go on."

"I came out on the beach, the access road leads directly to the beach . . ."

"Yes?"

"And I walked on the beach for a while."

"Still carrying the knife?"

"Let me think."

"Take your time."

"I must have thrown it in the water."

"In the Gulf?"

"Yes. While I was walking along, I threw it in the Gulf."

"Then what?"

"I sat down and began crying. In a little while, I got up and walked back toward the pine forest. There's a small gazebo just off the beach—the association had it built, there's a table there and benches on either side of it. I climbed up on the table and stretched out with my hands behind my head. I was planning to sleep there, I guess. I hadn't figured things out yet. I didn't know what I was going to do."

"About what, do you mean?"

"About . . . Maureen being dead. And the girls. I didn't know whether to . . . to go to the police and tell them I'd done it, or . . . just see what happened. I didn't want to go to the police, I was afraid they'd beat me up or . . ."

"But no one here has abused you physically or—"

"No, no."

"Mentally."

"No, everyone's been . . . it's just that you hear stories about the police. And this was . . . I thought they might have . . . you know . . . thought I'd . . . you know . . . done something to . . . Maureen."

"What do you mean by 'done something'?"

"Well, you know."

"Could you explain what you mean?"

"You know."

"I'm not sure."

"You know, her being in a nightgown and all."

"Yes, what about that?"

"The police might have got the idea I'd *done* something to her. Like, you know, molested her or something."

"*Did* you molest her?"

"No, sir. No, I didn't."

"You held her in your arms, though. You embraced her."

"Yes, but I didn't . . . you know . . . I didn't do . . . I didn't do what the police might *think* I'd done if I . . .

if I went to them and told them . . . told them . . . what I'd done."

"You embraced Emily, too, isn't that so?"

"Yes, but I didn't . . ."

"Go on. I'm listening."

"Didn't *do* anything to her."

"But you were afraid the police would *think* you'd done something to her."

"That's right."

"Something sexual?"

"Yes."

"But you didn't."

"No, sir, I did not."

"Not to Emily or to Maureen."

"She was . . . you know . . . the nightgown was all torn."

"Maureen's nightgown."

"Yes, but I didn't do anything to her, I swear to God."

"And the reason you didn't go to the police at first—"

"They might think I'd done something."

"You were afraid they'd think you had sexually abused her."

"Yes."

"Maureen."

"Yes."

"And that they'd beat you up if they found out."

"If they found out, yes. If they *thought* I'd done it, do you understand?"

"Mr. Purchase, why did you kill Maureen?"

"I don't know why."

"Why did you kill Emily?"

"I don't know."

"Or Eve?"

"I don't know."

"Mr. Purchase, I'm going to turn off the tape recorder now, and have this interview typed up in transcript form for you to read before you sign it. At that time, if you want to change anything or add anything to it, you can do so. In the meantime, *before* I turn off the machine, is there anything you'd like to add to your statement?"

"Nothing."

"Then that's everything," Ehrenberg said.

8

JAMIE AND I got back to my office at a little before one-thirty. I was ravenously hungry, but I didn't want to have lunch with him, and so I said nothing about it. His personal tragedy had lurched into the realm of genuine horror. I was numb and wanted no more of him or his son for a little while at least. I got out of the Ghia, and walked to where he was parking his car. Immediately, he began talking about Michael. Listening, I had the same feeling I'd had in that two A.M. bar last night—that he was talking to himself, soliciting my nods or my grunts only as punctuation to what was essentially a monologue.

"I thought he was over it by now," he said. "He was at the house only last Tuesday, he and Maureen sat at the kitchen table half the night, just talking. A real heart-to-heart talk. About my having stopped the alimony payments, about his going back to school—they'd have gone on forever if I hadn't told them I was going to bed, I had a busy day tomorrow."

Tomorrow would have been Wednesday. And Jamie would most certainly have had a busy day in the cottage at the beach. On Tuesday night, nonetheless, his son Michael sat at the kitchen table and had a long heart-to-heart talk with Maureen. This did not sound like someone who five days later would sit at that same table and abruptly reach for a knife.

"He was the one it hit hardest, you know," Jamie said. "He was only ten when I left his mother, it took me a full year and a half to reach an agreement with her, she made things miserable for all of us." He opened the door, climbed in behind the wheel. "But you know," he said, "I really thought he was over it. Came down here to live in September, started at U.S.F. . . . well, all right, he dropped out again in January, but I honestly think he was planning to start again in the fall. I honestly think he was beginning to . . . respect me again. Love me again."

Jamie shook his head. He was not looking at me. His hands were on the steering wheel, he was staring through the windshield at the bright white wall that surrounded the office complex.

"Then this afternoon, alone in the office with him, I said, 'Michael, why'd you do this? Michael, for the love of God, why'd you do this?' And he looked at me, and he said, 'It's your fault, Pop, *you* caused it,' and that was when I called him a son of a bitch, a little son of a bitch, and grabbed him by the throat. Because he was . . . he was right back where we'd been, don't you see? He was ten years old again, and blaming me again, only this time he was blaming me for the terrible thing he himself had done—it was *my* fault, he told me, *I* was the one who'd caused it. Matt, I . . . wanted to kill him. I was ready to kill him. If Ehrenberg hadn't come in . . . I'd have done it. God forgive me, I'd have done it."

The moment I stepped into the office, Cynthia said, "Galatier was here."

"I thought I asked you to cancel."

"I did. He came anyway."

"All right, get him for me. No, just a second, order me a sandwich and a bottle of beer first. *Then* call Galatier."

"What kind of sandwich?"

"Ham on rye, I don't care, anything."

"There's a list of calls on your desk."

"Fine, where's Frank?"

"At First Federal. The Kellerman closing."

"Hurry with the sandwich, I'm dying."

I went into my office, took off my jacket, and loosened my tie. There had been a dozen calls while I was gone, only one of them urgent. I assumed Frank had dealt with that one, since it had to do with the closing at First Federal. The bank had called to say that the interest rate had just been reduced by a quarter of a percent, and they were willing to permit the lower rate if we could change the papers before closing. The call had been clocked in at twelve-thirty, and the closing had been set for one-thirty. I picked up the phone and buzzed Cynthia.

"I ordered it already," she said. "They were all out of rye, I settled for white."

"Good. Cynthia, on this call from First Federal about the interest rate . . ."

"Frank dictated the changes, and I typed them for him before he left. Promissory note, mortgage, *and* closing statement. That was nice of the bank, don't you think?"

"Yes. When the sandwich arrives—"

"I'll bring it right in."

"Who saw Galatier when he was here?"

"Karl offered to talk to him, but he refused. Said he wouldn't deal with an office boy."

"All right, get him for me, please."

Cynthia came in ten minutes later with my ham sandwich and beer. Eating the sandwich, sipping beer from the bottle, I gave her a list of calls I wanted her to make, starting with Mrs. Joan Raal to tell her we'd be free of the lunatic Galatier come morning, and ending with Luis Camargo who was buying an apartment building we'd had examined for him by an engineer. The engineer had called while I was out, to say he'd found both the boiler *and* the electrical system deficient. I wanted Cynthia to ask Luis whether he still wanted to buy, or would he insist that the seller repair at his own expense.

"Is that it?" Cynthia asked.

"Yes. I'll be leaving here in a few minutes. I may be back later, but I'm not sure."

"Where can we reach you?"

"You won't be able to," I said. "I'll be on a boat."

Afternoon sunlight slanted on the water, reflected glaringly from white-painted pilings and slips. A pelican preened itself on one of the pilings, and then squinched down into the shape of a saucer. I came around the back of the restaurant, and walked past the row of docked boats jutting out into the lagoon. *The Broadhorn* was the fourth in line, her stern in against the dock, her name lettered on the transom in gold. I estimated her to be a forty-five-footer, maybe fifteen years old, a solid offshore cruiser with a blue wooden hull and white superstructure. I walked halfway up the slip, stopped just short of the wheelhouse and tentatively called, "Miss Schellmann?"

"Who is it?" a girl's voice answered.

"Matthew Hopc," I said. Silence. Water slapped against the boat's sides. "I'd like to talk to you about Michael Purchase." More silence. Out across the lagoon, in the mangroves, a tern shrieked and another answered, and then both were still. I could see down the dock to where a man in bright red pants was fishing, a bait knife hanging from his belt. I thought of the knife that had killed Maureen and the two children, the knife Michacl later threw into thc Gulf of Mexico. I waited.

"Who's Matthew Hope?" the girl said.

"Dr. Purchase's attorney."

Another silence.

"Come aboard," she said at last. "I'm on the foredeck."

I climbed onto the boat and eased down the narrow passage past the wheelhouse. Lisa Schellmann was lying prone on an inflated blue mat, her face turned to the left, her eyes closed. I saw her only in profile, slender nose faintly tip-tilted, wide upper lip beaded with perspiration, pronounced cheekbone slanting away cleanly into her blonde hairline. She was wearing a white bra top, the straps untied to show a wide expanse of brown back glistening with suntan oil. The swift line of her jaw curved into a flowing neck and shoulder, expanded into the smooth shining back, tapered to a narrow waist. Blue denim cut-offs began just in time to rescue the cleft of her behind.

"Miss Schellmann?" I said.

"Don't tell me," she said. Her eyes were still closed, her face still in profile on the blue mat. "Dr. Purchase wants the boat back, right?"

"No. Michael's in trouble."

The single eye opened. Pale blue against the deeper blue of the mat. "What do you mean, trouble?" she said.

"He's in jail."

"Why?"

"He's been charged with murder."

She sat up abruptly, swiveling cross-legged on the mat to face me, crossing one arm over the bikini top to keep it from falling away from her breasts. Her face was what Frank would most certainly have labeled a fox face, lean and narrow, a trifle too hard-looking for someone who couldn't have been older than eighteen. Pale blue eyes and long blonde lashes. Frizzy blonde hair sitting her skull like a knitted wool cap. She looked at me and said nothing.

"Yes," I said.

"Who? What do you . . . *who'd* he kill?"

"His stepmother and his two—"

"Jesus!" Lisa said, and stood abruptly, pushing herself off the mat from her cross-legged position. She turned her back to me, quickly tied the straps of the bikini top, and then reached for a brown leather bag resting on the deck near the starboard ventilator. She threw back the scroll-work flap, and dug in the bag for a pack of cigarettes. Her hand was shaking when she plucked one loose, put it between her lips, and lighted it. She tossed the burnt match over the side. Beyond, to the east, a sailboat was coming into the lagoon under power, her sails furled. She motored in past the bow of *The Broadhorn,* water sliding smoothly past her own bow.

"Tell me what happened," Lisa said.

"I've told you. Michael confessed to killing—"

"That's total bullshit."

"Why do you say that?"

"Michael? He couldn't," she said. "He's the gentlest person in the world."

"How long have you known him?"

"Two months. I've been living with him since January. I came for the Christmas break, and decided to stay."

"How old are you, Lisa?"

"Seventeen"

"Where were you living before you met Michael?"

"With my mother. My parents are divorced," she said.

"Where does your mother live?"

"Connecticut."

"And your father?"

"New York."

"Do they know where you are?" I asked.

"They know where I am, yes," she said, and flipped the cigarette over the side. It hissed into the water. Some three slips down, the sailboat had maneuvered in, and a woman in an orange bikini was making the dock lines fast.

"Michael told the police he needed money," I said. "To make a repair on the boat. Would you know anything about that?"

"He was probably talking about the oil leak."

"Yes, what about it?"

"We're losing drive oil. Michael first noticed it on the gauge, the needle kept dropping down to fifty or sixty. Then he checked the dipstick, and put in more oil, but it just leaked out again. It's a big job to fix it. They've got to jack the engine up on an A-frame and put in a new gasket, and I think replace the plate. The marina gave him an estimate of six hundred dollars. That's more than both of us make together in a month."

"Where do you work, Lisa?"

"At the Cross River Market. I'm a checker."

"And Michael?"

"He's a busboy at Leonardo's."

"Was he working yesterday?"

"No, Sunday's his day off."

"Was he here on the boat then?"

"Yes."

"All day?"

"Well, he left late at night."

"Where was he going?"
"I don't know."
"Did you ask him?"
"Yes. He just said he'd be back in a little while."
"What time was this?"
"Right after he got the phone call. It must've been—"
"*What* phone call?"
"Somebody called him."
"Here on the boat? There's a phone on the boat?"
"No, up at the dockmaster's office. He'll come get us if it isn't too late."
"What time was it?"
"About eleven-thirty."
"Who was calling?"
"I don't know."
"Did you ask Michael?"
"Yes."
"What did he say?"
"He said it was nothing important. Then he went below, and got his wallet from the dresser and came topside again. That's when I asked him where he was going, and he said he'd be back in a little while."
"When the dockmaster came to get him . . . did *he* say who was on the phone?"
"He just said, 'There's a call for you, Mike.' He likes Michael a lot, he won't believe this. He just won't believe it."
"Were you worried when Michael didn't come back?"
"No, I wasn't worried. I mean, I didn't think anything had *happened* to him. I thought maybe he'd met some girl, you know, and decided to stay with her for the night. I guess that's what I thought. Because, you see, we have an understanding like if I meet some boy I want to know better, I can do that, you see, and it's the same with him, with a girl, I mean. I can leave this boat any time I want to, I can just pack up and go. That's our understanding."
"Who ordinarily pays for the boat's maintenance?"
"I don't understand what you mean."
"If something goes wrong with the boat, does Michael pay to have it repaired, or does his father?"
"Well, normally Michael, I guess. I really don't know,

I never asked him about who paid for what. But Michael puts in the gas, and he pays for keeping the boat here, it costs two-fifty a foot, plus sixty-five for the power cord. It comes to a hundred eighty-five a month, something like that. Michael does all the minor repairs himself, but this is a big job, this oil leak, so I guess he would've asked his father to pay for it, if that's what you mean."

"But Michael said he went there to *borrow* the money."

"Well, maybe so. He's got a lot of pride. His father thinks of him as nothing but a plastic hippie, that's because Michael's having trouble finding himself, you know. But he's got a lot of pride and I can see him only asking for a loan and not for the money as a gift. I know it bothered Michael that he was living on the boat freebies, that his father was letting him use the boat, you know? He kept telling me he wanted to buy a boat of his own. But in the meantime, you know, his father never went out on it, Maureen would get seasick even if it was just the bay, never mind the Gulf. So he offered the boat to Michael to live on, and Michael said sure why not?" Lisa shrugged elaborately. "But I know it bothered him. Because they've had hassles, you know. Michael's not a bum, you know, he's just having trouble getting his head together; in fact, he's been talking about going back to school, I think he's really seriously considering it. That's something you ought to know because . . . I mean, how *could* he have killed her? I mean, why *would* he have killed her?"

"I'm sorry, I don't understand you."

"Well, it was *Maureen* who was encouraging him to go back. I mean, *I* don't care if he goes back or not, whatever makes him happy. But Maureen was the one talking about his future, and about did he want to be a busboy all his life? They really got along fine, he respected her a lot, he really did. There was a conflict there for him, you know, he felt guilty about relating to Maureen when he had a mother of his own. But Michael found it difficult to talk to either of his parents because of all the trouble—"

"What do you mean? What trouble?"

"Well, you know, all the hard feelings about the divorce. It isn't easy, you know, take it from me. Michael was only ten when his father split, twelve when he finally married Maureen. Those are tough years for a kid *anyway,* never mind divorce. And his mother didn't make it any easier, told both kids their father had been playing around with half the women in town, made Maureen out to be just another tramp, you know, like that. What I'm saying is Michael gave his father a pretty rough time, and I'm not sure his father's forgotten it yet."

"What kind of a rough time?"

"Well, like I just told you."

"You only said there were hard feelings about the divorce."

"Well, yeah, but . . . like the time in Virginia. You probably know about it."

"No. Tell me."

"Well, she sent Michael away to a military academy—"

"Yes, I know that."

"And he got caught smoking pot there, the general caught him smoking pot. He was about sixteen at the time, the general refused to let him go home for the spring break—the spring furlough, he called it. So Michael's father went all the way to Virginia to see him, and Michael just wouldn't give him the right time, told him to go to hell."

"He actually said that?"

"No, but he told his father he was doing fine without him."

"What else?"

"Well, you know about the trip to India . . ."

"No."

"Well, Michael started school at U.C.L.A.—this was after he got out of that place in Virginia—and then he dropped out of there and went first to Amsterdam and then India, and Afghanistan, I think it was, or Pakistan, one of those countries. He was following the drug route, you know, he got into drugs pretty heavy in Amsterdam—"

"He's not involved in drugs now, is he?"

"No, no," Lisa said. "He was never into the hard stuff, anyway. He's never put a needle in his arm. He never would. He may have sniffed coke while he was in Europe, I don't know about that, he was traveling with a junkie in

Denmark. But what I meant was acid, he got into acid in Holland. And, of course, pot, But everybody smokes pot," she said, and shrugged. "The point is, he never wrote to his father all that time. He had the man going crazy, he admits that now. Sending letters to the American Embassy, writing to Washington, while Michael's climbing the Himalayas and sniffing flowers and having his hair and his beard dyed red by mountain priests. He used to write his father about the spiders in the hut he lived in. Big spiders. Told him about the spiders to make him worry even more, that was all. Never a return address on the letters. *I'm in the mountains,* period. *With priests and spiders.* Lots of mountains there, man." Lisa shook her head. "What I'm saying is the relationship with his father was strained, you know what I mean? It was getting better, but it was still strained."

"How about his mother?"

"How about her? Have you ever met her?"

"I've met her."

"Then you know. A fat pain in the ass. Always using Michael as a messenger boy—tell your father this, tell him that. Phoning him three, four times a week, sending him letters. He was fed up to here with her."

"So he talked to Maureen instead."

"Well, he talked to *me,* too," Lisa said, "but that's different. I mean, we're lovers."

I looked at her.

She was seventeen years old, another child of divorce, mother in Connecticut, father in New York—or was it the other way around? Her parents knew where she was, she'd said, and thrown her cigarette over the side—as abruptly as her parents had thrown *her* over the side—or so she must have thought or felt. "They know where I am, yes," the cigarette hissing into the water with the sibilance of the final "yes," the silence echoing with the unspoken corollary, "And don't *give* a damn."

I wanted to ask her . . . I wanted to say . . . I wanted to talk about the divorce of *her* parents. I wanted to know how she'd reacted—when had it been, how old were you, Lisa, which of your parents asked for the divorce, was there another woman involved? Do you ever see your parents, Lisa, do you ever see your *father?* What kind of person is he, do you love him and respect him, do you love him? Have you forgiven him for leaving? Will you ever? I looked into her eyes and into a future I could scarcely imagine, no less hope to comprehend. My future. My daughter's.

"Is Michael allowed visitors?" she asked.

"Not yet," I said.

"Where is he now?"

"They're holding him at the police station. He probably won't be moved across the street till tomorrow morning."

"But he's in jail, you said."

"Yes. At the police station. They have cells there."

"I wonder . . ."

"Yes, Lisa?"

"What I should do now? I mean . . . where should I go?"

The dockmaster's office at Pirate's Cove was just adjacent to the motel office, the pair of white entrance doors set side by side in an otherwise red-shingled structure. I knocked on the door, got no answer, tried the knob, and found the door locked. I went into the motel office, and asked the woman behind the desk there where I could find the dockmaster. She said he was outside someplace. I went outside again, circled the building, and saw a grizzled old man bent over a bed of geraniums, turning the sandy earth around them with a trowel. He was wearing a battered, soiled yachting cap tilted low over one eye, a striped T-shirt, blue jeans and scuffed topsiders.

"Excuse me, sir?" I said.

"Yes, sir," he said, but did not look up from the flowerbed.

"I'm looking for the dockmaster," I said.

"You've found him," he said.

"I'm Matthew Hope."

"Donald Wicherly," he said, and rose abruptly. "What can I do for you?"

"I'd like to ask you some questions about a phone call you took last night."

"Why?" he said. His eyes were the color of the sky

behind him, squinched now and studying me suspiciously. The hand holding the trowel was on his hip, he stood in angular expectation, a tall, lean, weathered man wanting to know why I had questions, and probably wondering besides why he should answer them.

"I'm an attorney," I told him. "I'm here about Michael Purchase."

"You're Michael's attorney?"

"Yes. Well, actually, I'm his father's attorney."

"Which is it then? Michael's attorney or his father's?"

"His father's. But I'm here on Michael's behalf."

"With Michael's knowledge or without it?"

"He knows I'm here," I said. I was lying, but I wanted information, and I was beginning to resent this examination before trial. "Michael got a phone call last night," I said. "About eleven-thirty. You took the call."

"Are you asking me or telling me?"

"*Did* you take the call?"

"I took it."

"Where would that have been?"

"In the office,"

"Who called him?"

"I don't know. The party didn't identify herself."

"It was a woman?"

"A woman, yes."

"Could you make a guess at her age?"

"Well, no, sir, I don't think I could."

"Can you tell me what she said?"

"She asked if this was Pirate's Cove, and I said it was. She said could she please speak to Michael Purchase? I told her he was down on the boat, and I'd have to go fetch him. She said would I do that please, and I went down to get him."

"Then what?"

"He came up to the office with me, and talked to her on the phone."

"Did you hear the conversation?"

"Only the tail end of it. I'd gone back to my apartment for something I wanted to staple on the bulletin board. He was still talking when I came into the office again."

"What did you hear?"

"He said 'I'll be right there,' then he said 'Good-bye,' and hung up."

"You didn't hear him mention anyone's name?"

"No, sir, I did not."

"Did he say anything to you after he hung up?"

"He said, 'Thank you, Mr. Wicherly.' "

"That's all?"

"Yes, sir."

"He didn't say where he was going, did he?"

"No, but I'd guess he was going to where he told that woman he'd be going." He paused. He looked into my eyes. "According to what I heard on the radio about what he's supposed to have done, why then he'd have gone straight to the house on Jacaranda to kill the three of them. That's where he'd have gone, and that's what he'd have done." He shook his head. "But I'll tell you, Mr. Hope, I find that mighty hard to believe. I just don't *know* any boy nicer than Michael Purchase, that's the truth. His parents got divorced when he was just twelve, you know . . . well, I guess you know that, you're his father's attorney."

"Yes, I know that."

"That ain't an easy thing for a young boy. We had a long talk about it one night. Told me he was finally coming through it, after all these years. So you see, when I hear on the radio he killed his father's wife and his two sisters . . . those girls were his *sisters,* Mr. Hope, there was his father's blood in *them* and in Michael both, the same blood. Whenever he talked about them, they were his sisters, never mind half sisters. His sisters this, his sisters that, he could have been talking about his full sister, that's all a lot of crap, anyway, isn't it? It's how you feel about somebody that counts. He loved those little girls. And you don't do what the radio says he done if you love somebody. You just don't."

But he said he did, I reminded myself.

9

FROM A phone booth in the marina restaurant, I called Ehrenberg and told him I'd like to talk to Michael Purchase as soon as possible. He said the boy was still being processed and asked if I could make it a little later in the afternoon.

"What do you mean by 'processed'?" I said.

"Putting him through the booking facility. Photographing him, printing him, taking hair clippings, blood samples—we're allowed to do that, counselor, he's been charged with Murder One. We'll be sending everything up to the state lab in Tallahassee. I don't know how long it'll take for them to compare the boy's hair with what we vacuumed off the woman and the two girls. Might be nothing there at all, who knows? I'm betting the blood on his clothes is theirs, though." He sounded glum. He paused, and then said, "What did you think of his statement?"

"I don't know what to think."

"Neither do I."

"When can I see him?"

"Can you give us till four-thirty?"

"I'll be there," I said, and hung up. I took another dime from my pocket, inserted it into the coin slot, and dialed

Aggie's number. She was breathless when she answered the phone.

"I was on the beach," she said. "I came running up to the house. Where are you, Matt?"

"The restaurant at Pirate's Cove. Are you still alone?"

"Yes."

"Can I come there?"

"Now?"

"Yes."

She hesitated. Then she said, "All right. Park at the public beach, and come up on the ocean side."

"I'll be there by three," I said.

"I'll be waiting."

We both knew it was reckless; we didn't give a damn. Calusa in season is not designed for lovers. Aggie and I had first begun seeing each other in May, almost a year ago. The tourists had left shortly after Easter, and we'd had no difficulty finding places where we could be alone together. But just before Christmas the shrill cry of the snowbird was heard upon the air again—and from Tampa south to Fort Myers the neon NO VACANCY signs crackled and sputtered like a single unbroken electrified fence. In January, we stole a weekend together in Tarpon Springs, and then returned to a city still overrun with tourists; everytime I saw a CALUSA LOVES TOURISTS bumper sticker, I wanted to honk for Jesus. I went to Aggie's house for the first time that month, and I'd been going there at least once a week since, sometimes more often. It was at the beginning of February that we decided we would ask for separate divorces. We made the decision because we weren't true adulterers. We were, instead, people who'd happened to fall in love with each other while we were married to . . .

Ah, yes, the judge would say, you're just a pair of decent souls, poor innocent babes in the woods who've been humping your brains out for the past ten months in this or that motel and even in the lady's own *house*, lying and cheating and stealing, yes, stealing! That's exactly what you've been doing, you cannot look me in the eye and pretend you've not been stealing. And I'm not referring only to the *time* you steal in this or that trysting place, those steamy hours you spend together in embrace, oh no.

I'm referring as well to the intangibles you swipe from your separate spouses: the trust, the love, the honor you granted them by contract and which you now burglarize as unconscionably as thieves in the night. You *are* all those things, the both of you; you are liars, cheats, and thieves.

And I would say Yes, your Honor, you're right.

But you see, that's exactly the point.

I folded my jacket on the back seat of the Ghia and then took off my tie and unbuttoned the two top buttons of my shirt. I left my shoes and socks on the passenger seat up front, locked the car, and crossed the parking lot to the beach. There were bathers in the water despite the shark scare on the east coast. Sandpipers skirted the shoreline, gulls shrieked overhead. Out on the Gulf, a Hobie cat with a red-and-white striped sail glided soundlessly over the waves.

Aggie's house on Whisper Key was built some two hundred yards back from the water's edge, powdery white sand turning coarser as the beach vaguely became the western approach, tall grass springing out of the sand, palm trees in clusters, a path of round irregularly spaced stepping stones leading to the rear wall of the house. The house stood on stilts, a contemporary two-story structure of weathered gray cypress and large glass areas that now reflected the midafternoon sun. An old lady in a flowered housedress was shelling just at the shoreline. Her head was bent, she did not look up as I veered off the beach, and walked through the palms toward the screened pool area on the lower level.

I was always glad to see her. I told her once that this was how I knew I loved her; I was always very glad to see her. An almost boyish gladness. A grin I could not suppress. An irresistible desire to hug her. I did that now, the moment I stepped into the tiled and shaded corridor where she waited for me. Grinning, I hugged her, and kissed her closed eyes and kissed her mouth briefly and held her away from me and looked at her.

She was wearing a white bikini, her skin tan against it, except for a narrow line of paler flesh just above the bra top. Long black hair combed as sleekly straight as Cleopatra's, gray eyes, a mouth perhaps too generous for her face, an almost perfect nose, tiny white scar above the bridge. Sometimes, away from her, I conjured images I thought were surely false—her hair couldn't possibly be as black as I imagined it, her eyes so pale, her smile so radiant. And then I'd be with her again, and my pleasure at simply *seeing* her would give way in an instant to the shock of recognizing once again how extraordinarily beautiful she truly was.

I put my arm around her waist, resting my spread hand on her hip, and we walked together through the familiar tiled hallway, past tall potted ferns in white tubs, and up a circular staircase set with dark wooden pie-shaped steps in black wrought iron. A window here leaped vertically tall and narrow to the west, ablaze with orange now as the sun hovered midway between ocean and universe. The guest room was on the topmost level of the house, one windowed wall angled somewhat less than due west to catch the sunset and at the same time lessen the glare. The other wall faced an inland lagoon crowded with marsh grass, a sandy beach coming to the eastern side of the house where sea grape fanned out over a slatted wooden wall.

We had come long past examining what we did here in this house together while her husband and children were away from it. Aggie took off her bikini the moment we were in the room, and I undressed swiftly and then we lay side by side on the bed and shamelessly made love. The orange glow on the vertical where we'd left the door purposely ajar in order to hear any unexpected sounds from below. Her mouth tasted of salt.

We talked afterwards in whispers, exchanging at first bedroom banalities, assuring and reassuring, the universal clichès—*Was it good? Yes, was it good for you, too?* Aggie lit a cigarette and sat in the middle of the bed cross-legged, smoking, a small ashtray cupped in her left hand. I do not smoke; I haven't smoked for seven years. I watched her. The pink flush of sex was fading across the wings of her collarbones and the sloping tops of her breasts. A fine sheen of perspiration was on her face, the hair at her temples was damp. She asked me if the tennis elbow was giving me trouble again and I told her it was, and asked how she knew. She immediately described in detail an acrobatic maneuver we'd performed not three minutes before, and mimicked the way I'd winced while shifting my weight. I began to chuckle. She told me she loved the way I laughed, and then bent from the waist and impulsively kissed me. The clock on the dresser was ticking away the afternoon.

We were acutely aware of the time. There was so much to say to each other, but the clock read 3:47 and each tick brought us closer to that dangerous uncertain area of surprise discovery. Monday was Julie's day for guitar. Her father would be picking her up at four-thirty, by which time I would have left his house and his wife. Gerald, Jr., was on his school's basketball team, and would be driven home from practice by one of the mothers in the car pool. He was not expected till just before dusk. We seemed to be safe. But there was a knife-edged tension in the air.

Aggie was thirty-four years old. She complained constantly about the waste of her education and her training—she'd graduated summa cum laude from Radcliffe and was doing psychiatric social work in Boston when she met her husband. She was twenty-three at the time. She married him a year later and quit working when she was six months pregnant with Julie. So now she railed against dishwashers and car pools, dealing with three-day-a-week help, the long empty hours of wife and mother. But at the same time, she was cruel in examining her own hedonistic life, and was the first to admit that she *adored* the luxury of being able to play tennis when the kids were at school, or take long walks on the beach, or simply sit in the sun and read. Yes, Aggie loved the laziness and the freedom, she admitted that, yes. But if *I* tried to suggest that she enjoyed it, she immediately accused me of holding sexist views.

I once told her a long story about this North Vietnamese pilot who was flying a Russian-made airplane painted gray. He was possibly the best pilot the North Vietnamese had, but when it was rumored that the Americans might be putting *women* pilots into their warplanes and sending them up against him, he absolutely refused to fly any more combat missions. His gray Russian-made airplane was grounded for the rest of the war, and whenever American pilots flew over it, they pointed it out to each other.

"And do you know what they called it, Aggie?"

"I don't know. What did they call it?"

"The Pale Chauvinist MIG."

"Very funny, ha-ha."

She took her role as a woman seriously. Whenever I suggested to her that perhaps she'd begun this affair with me only because she was restless, she told me not to cheapen what we shared, and then immediately said, "Of *course,* I'm restless. You'd be restless, too, if you had nothing to do but *enjoy* yourself all day long!"

She told me now of the play she'd been rehearsing with the Whisper Key Players, an amateur dramatics group. She was having difficulty with the director. At rehearsal this morning, he'd shrieked at her to *please,* for the love of *God,* speak *up!* She was hoarse with shouting by that point; she glared at him across the rows of empty seats and advised him to go buy a hearing aid. The rest of the cast began laughing, and the director said, "Cute, Aggie, very cute," and stormed out of the theater. She felt awful about it now, and wanted to know what I thought she should do. The man simply did not return. Should she call him to apologize? The play had been in rehearsal for three weeks, it was scheduled to open this Saturday night—would I come to the opening?

I told her I didn't see how I possibly could; what plausible reason could I give Susan for wanting to see a play done by an amateur group? Aggie laughed and said, "You mean *The Plough and the Stars* isn't your favorite play in the entire world?" Her laughter was a bit forced, I couldn't at first understand why. She'd never taken the group seriously, and her role in the play was a minor one. We had, in fact, joked about her finally accepting the part.

"I play a prostitute," she'd said. "Do you think that's typecasting?"

"Why'd you take it?"

"Nancy kept bugging me. Besides, I'll get to show a lot of leg and garter," she'd said, and winked.

But now she was silent, her eyes brooding, her mouth set. I asked her what was wrong, and she told me again what I'd heard at least a dozen times before. The thrust of her argument (it was really a plea) was that I did not value her highly enough. It was *Susan* I cared about, *Susan* who rated my concern—what plausible reason could I give *Susan* for wanting to see a play done by a bunch of amateurs, right?

"The hell with Susan," she said, "what about *me?* What plausible reason can you give *me* for not coming to see a play I'm in?"

"I didn't know the play was that important to you."

"It isn't. Why didn't you tell her last night?"

"What?"

"When I spoke to you on the phone this morning—"

"Oh, I see, this goes all the way back to this morning."

"Yes, *all* the way back. You said—"

"I know what I said."

"You said you'd almost told her last night. Why *almost,* Matt?"

"Because the phone rang and it was—"

"If it hadn't been the phone . . ."

"It *was* the phone. It was, in fact—"

"Matt, you've been on the verge of telling her for the past month now. Each time, something stops you. The phone rings, the cat pees on the kitchen floor, it's always —now what the hell's so funny, would you mind telling me?"

"The cat peeing on the kitchen floor."

"I don't find any of this funny, I'm sorry. I'm beginning to think you enjoy having a wife *and* a whore you can fuck every Wednesday!"

"This is Monday."

"Matt, this isn't funny. If you don't *want* to tell Susan about us, I wish you'd—"

"I *do* want to tell her."

"Then why haven't you already . . . oh the *hell* with it!" she said, and pushed herself off the bed, and stalked angrily across the room, her bare feet slapping against the tiled floor. I looked at the clock. The minute hand visibly lurched another minute past the hour, startling me. The clock was ticking furiously, the afternoon was sliding downhill. I wanted to settle this with her, I loved her too much to leave her in an agitated state. But I wanted to get back to the mainland before Ehrenberg left for the day, and I was also—I admitted this to myself with a faint pang—afraid that Gerald Hemmings would walk into his house and find me naked with his naked wife. I went to Aggie where she was standing at the window, her arms crossed over her waist, her hands cupping opposite elbows. I took her in my arms.

"Aggie, I don't know why we're fighting."

"I think you know why."

"Tell me."

"For a simple reason. You don't love me. That's why we're fighting."

"I love you."

"Get dressed," she said. "Its late, Matt."

I dressed silently. She watched from the window as I buttoned my shirt. Then she said, "I won't ask you again, Matt. You'll tell her when you want to. *If* you want to."

"I'll tell her tonight."

"Sure," she said, and smiled wanly. The smile frightened me more than anything she'd said. I had the feeling that something was about to end without warning. "A long time ago, I asked you if you were sure," she said. "The first time in the motel. Do you remember?"

"Yes. And I told you I was."

"Be sure this time, too, Matt."

"Are *you* sure?"

"Yes, darling," she said, and looked suddenly exhausted. I pulled her to me and held her very tight.

"You'd better go," she said. "It's very late."

"I'll tell her tonight."

"Don't promise."

"I promise."

We kissed. I moved my face back from hers and looked at her again. She seemed about to speak, and hesitated, and then at last said, "Every time you leave me to go back to her, I think it'll be forever. I'm always surprised when you're here the next time. I'm even surprised when you call again."

"I love you, Aggie."

"Do you?"

She smiled again. The smile suddenly appeared and faded at once. Her pale gray eyes searched my face. I kissed her once more and then turned away and started for the door. In the hallway outside, the vertical window had become a column of blood.

The second-floor corridor was long and narrow, constructed of cinderblock painted a yellowish beige. An overhead water pipe ran arrow-straight down one side of the corridor, and an overhead duct hung from the ceiling on the opposite side. The corridor was lighted artificially, the plastic-covered ceiling fixtures spaced regularly along its length between the exposed water pipe and the duct. A water cooler bisected the corridor on the right hand side. There were open doors on that same wall, casting a greenish light into the otherwise mustard gloom.

Ehrenberg had met me ten minutes ago on the first floor of the building, and then walked me around to a flight of steps that led upstairs to the holding cells. A jailer let us onto the second floor, and then disappeared into his office to answer a ringing telcphone. The door at the far end of the corridor was made of metal; I could make that out even from this distance. A small rectangular glass panel was set into the door at eye level. The metal plate surrounding the keyway was painted a bright red. It seemed the only patch of color in the corridor. There was a sense here of stone and steel, an architecture of necessity. This was a jail. It looked like a jail, even though I had not yet seen a cell.

We were waiting outside the room used for photographing and fingerprinting prisoners. I could see inside to where a camera was mounted on a makeshift wooden frame to which a spot light was fastened above. On the wall opposite the camera, there was a chair and above the chair there was a combination electric clock and digital day-date indicator. The hands of the clock read 4:38. The date read MAR 1, the day read MON. Presumably Michael had been sitting in that chair just a short while ago, his picture being taken below a pair of instruments that recorded the day, the time and the place, and assigned to him a number besides.

"Detective Di Luca had a chance to talk to a Miss Louise Verhaagen, if that's how she pronounces it," Ehrenberg said. "She's one of the nurses working for Dr. Purchase. I'll tell you what I was doing, Mr. Hope. I was operating on the theory that a man who lies about why he left a poker game and where he went afterwards is a man who's got a little bimbo he's keeping someplace. Do you remember when I asked Dr. Purchase was he fooling around outside the marriage? Well, he told me he was very happily married but he didn't exactly answer my question. So Di Luca talked to Miss Verhaagen this afternoon, shortly after you left here, and whereas she didn't precisely confirm my suspicion that the doctor was playing around, she didn't deny it either. In fact, she stated right out that there were a great many phone calls from a woman named Catherine Brenet, who it happens is not a patient, and who it further happens is a married lady who herself has a doctor for a husbnd. Well, okay, that doesn't mean Dr. Purchase went home and killed his wife and two daughters, it doesn't necessarily mean that at all. It could only mean he was out fooling around with this Mrs. Brenet while the murders were taking place, in which case I'm going to have to talk to the lady herself to find out if he was."

"Why?" I said.

"Why? What do you mean 'why'?"

"You've got a confession from the boy."

"Yes, I have, that's true. But there're some blanks in it that don't sit right with me. Whether you believe this or not, Mr. Hope, I'm not eager to send that young boy to the electric chair just on his say-so. Not with his mother and father both giving me alibis I can drive a truck through. We canvassed the mother's neighborhood like exterminators looking for bugs. House across the street from her is up for sale, no one there to see her coming or going. None of the neighbors saw any lights on that night, but she says she was watching television at the back of the house, so okay. But most of them seem to think the garage door was closed the *whole* day long. So I've got to ask was she *home* all day or was she *out* all day? I'm only speculating, Mr. Hope, but let's say she had it in her head to do murder, couldn't she have left the house five, six in the morning, spent the day doing God knows what, and then gone home two, three the *next* morning, without anyone being the wiser? I just don't know. I'm not finished with her yet, not by a long shot. Nor with the doctor, either. As for the boy . . . there's things make it sound like he did it, and things make it sound like he didn't. I still don't know why he suddenly reached up for that knife, do you?"

"No, I don't."

"Sitting there at the kitchen table, having a nice chat, when all of a sudden he grabs a knife and chases her in the bedroom. Can't give a reason for it." Ehrenberg shook his head. "That sounds peculiar to me, doesn't it to you?"

"Yes."

"At the same time, he starts stammering and stuttering about why he's afraid to go to the police, afraid of what they might think. Well, that makes me wonder did he sexually abuse that woman, and those two girls. Which might explain why he killed them. He's got no explanation for *why* he did it, you see. Now, there's plenty of cases where somebody blanks out, they just kill in a rage, they don't know why afterwards. But I still think this is peculiar, I really do. Unless he, you know, raped them. Or *tried* to rape them. He says he embraced the woman and the older daughter both, I just don't know what that means in terms of this case. You got any ideas?"

"No, I haven't," I said. I did not tell him that Michael had received a phone call at eleven-thirty last night, just before he'd gone to his father's house. That was what I was here to talk to Michael about.

"Because if he *didn't* sexually abuse them, why was he afraid the police would think so? I mean, if he'd *killed* somebody, for Christ's sake, why would he be worried about *hugging* them? You think he'd be more worried the police would say he'd done murder, am I right? I just don't understand it." Ehrenberg sighed heavily. "I'm going to have a talk with this Brenet woman—she owns and operates a flower shop here on South Bayview. See if the doctor really *was* with her last night. If he was, I can understand why he lied to me. Be some can of worms to open, wouldn't it?"

"Yes, it would."

"But it still wouldn't explain why the *boy* is lying. Well, I don't mean lying, I mean withholding the complete truth. There's a difference. Don't you get the feeling he's not telling the whole truth?"

"I don't know."

"Yeah," Ehrenberg said, and looked at his watch. "They're doing the autopsies now at Calusa Memorial, we'll know in a little while whether there was any injury to the genital organs, or any sperm inside the woman or the girls. The clothes we sent to Tallahassee'll be checked for vaginal stains might've come from the woman, I just don't *know* about this damn case. There're too many things—"

The jailer reappeared just then, apologizing for having kept us waiting so long. As he went down the corridor, he explained that his wife had called with a washing-machine problem. When we got to the steel door at the end of the corridor, he lifted a ring of keys from his belt, and fitted a key that was color-coded red into the keyway. He twisted it, and swung open the heavy door. There were suddenly bars. Bars multiplying one beyond the next, as in the mirrors of a fun-house. I was looking at a large cage with dividing bars that formed a series of cages within, each equipped with cots, sinks and toilets.

"This's the bull pen," the jailer said. "For the trustics."

We walked parallel to the bars, down a narrow corridor, made an abrupt right turn and came into a cul-de-sac at the end of which was a pair of cells. Michael was in the cell closest to the bend in the hallway. The jailer used the same color-coded key to open the door, red into red the color of blood. Michael was wearing prison clothing. Dark blue trousers, pale blue denim shirt, black shoes and socks. He was sitting on the single cot in the cell, his hands between his knees, just as he'd been sitting when first I saw him in his blood-stained garments in the captain's office. On the wall just inside the barred door, there was a white porcelain sink with two push-button faucets. Just beyond that was the toilet bowl, no seat on it, just the white porcelain bowl and a roll of toilet paper sitting on the neck of the bowl where it was fastened to the wall. On the mustard-colored wall to the right, a prisoner had penciled the words I NEED MENTAL REHABILITATION, misspelling the last word. Another prisoner had scratched his name onto the wall and alongside it had drawn a rectangle divided down the middle with a single line, perhaps as an intended replica of the twin cells here at the end of the hall. There was only an uncovered and extremely dirty foam rubber mattress on the wall-fastened cot. I stepped into the cell and felt immediately confined when the jailer locked the door behind me.

"Just yell when you want out," he said, and he and Ehrenberg went down the corridor, turned the corner of the L, and vanished. I heard the tumblers falling in the heavy steel door. The door squeaked open and clanged shut. The sound of the tumblers again. And then silence.

"How are you doing, Michael?" I said.

"Okay," he said.

"Are they treating you all right?"

"Fine. They cut off some of my hair, are they allowed to do that?"

"Yes."

"From around my cock, too. Why'd they do that?"

"Why do you think, Michael?"

"I don't know."

"They'll be making comparison tests."

"Of what?"

"Any hairs found on the bodies. They'll compare your hair against whatever they found."

"Why?"

"Michael, they want to know whether rape was a part of this."

"I told them it wasn't. I told them exactly what happened last night. What more do they—"

"You didn't tell them about the phone call."

"What phone call?"

"I went to the boat this afternoon. I spoke to Lisa Schellmann, she told me—"

"Lisa's a birdbrain."

"She said there was a phone call last night."

"There wasn't."

"Michael, the dockmaster took the call, he's already confirmed it. He went down to the boat to get you, and you went back with him to the office, and talked to the woman who—"

"I didn't talk to any woman."

"Are you telling me you did *not* get a phone call from a woman at eleven-thirty last night?"

"I didn't get a call from *any*body *any*time last night."

"Michael, that's a lie," I said.

He turned his head away.

"Why are you lying?"

"I'm not lying."

"A woman called you last night, the dockmaster'll swear to it. Now who was she?"

"Nobody."

"Michael, the dockmaster heard you saying you'd be right there. *Where* was right there, can you tell me that?"

"No place. The dockmaster heard wrong. Are you talking about Mr. Wicherly?"

"Yes."

"He's deaf. He's a deaf old man. How would he know what—"

"He's *not* deaf, Michael, he hears perfectly well. Where was right there?"

He hesitated.

"Michael?"

"The house," he said.

"Your father's house?"

"Yes."

"Who called you, Michael?"

He hesitated again.

"Michael, who . . . ?"

"Maureen. Maureen called me."

"What did she want?"

"She said she wanted to see me."

"What about?"

"She said to come over."

"Why?"

"She wanted to talk."

"Did she tell you your father was out?"

"She said there was . . . she said . . . the three of them were there."

"Maureen and your sisters?"

"The little girls."

"And she wanted you to come over?"

"Yes. She said she was . . . she was . . . she'd be waiting for me."

"All right, Michael, what happened when you got there? What did you talk about? You told Detective Ehrenberg you went into the kitchen—"

"Yes, that's right."

"What did you talk about?"

"I don't remember."

"Try to remember. Did she tell you why she wanted to see you?"

"She was scared."

"Why?"

"Of . . . she didn't know what to do."

"About what?"

"I don't know."

"But she told you she was scared?"

"Yes."

"Then what?"

"I don't remember."

"Did Maureen say something to anger you?"

"No, we . . . we always . . . we always got along fine. We . . . no."

"You just suddenly reached up for the knife and began chasing her through the house, is that it?"

"In the bedroom, I . . ."

"Yes, what happened in the bedroom?"

"I took her in my arms," he said. "I kissed her on the mouth."

"Yes, then what?"

"I didn't want the police to know I'd . . . I didn't want them to know I'd kissed . . . my father's wife. She was my father's wife, I'd kissed her."

"And you didn't want the police to know that?"
"No, I . . . they'd tell my father."
"Is that why you stabbed her?"
"No." He shook his head. "That was afterwards."
"Michael, I'm not following you."
"After she was dead."
"You kissed her after she was dead?"
"Yes."
"Is that what you didn't want the police to know?"
"Yes," he said.
"Did you kiss Emily, too?"
"No, just my mother."
"Your mother?"
"Maureen."

It was a little past five when I parked outside the flower shop. Ehrenberg hadn't given me the name of the place, but there was only one on South Bayview, and I had to assume this was the one Catherine Brenet owned and operated. I was aware of the fact that Susan and I were supposed to attend a gallery opening sometime between five and seven, but it seemed to me more important to talk to Mrs. Brenet before Ehrenberg got to her.

The shop was in a row of stores on the same side of the street as the Royal Palms Hotel. Turreted and balconied, shuttered and terraced, the hotel created for the entire street an aura of graciousness, reminiscent of what Calusa must have been like in the 1920's. All was quiet in the late afternoon sunlight. I could visualize horses and buggies coming down a palm-shaded esplanade, could imagine luxurious gardens stretching clear to the bay. The sidewalk in front of the flower shop was a miniature garden in itself. A potted umbrella tree stood side by side with a dragon tree and a corn plant, all arranged around a flower cart massed with purple, white and pink gloxinias, mums in yellow and lavender, spinning wheels with bright yellow centers and white petals. The plate glass window of the shop was lettered with the words LE FLEUR DE LIS over a heraldic crest showing a pair of stylized three-petaled irises. The name of the shop, coupled with the knowledge that it was owned by Jamie's mistress, whose name in turn was Catherine Brenet, somehow conspired to create the expectation of a French poule licking her lips seductively and asking, *"Desirez, monsieur?"*

There was only one person in the shop, a somewhat dumpy, middle-aged woman, blonde hair pulled into a severe bun at the back of her head, wearing oversized glasses with tortoise-shell frames, soil-stained green smock, the handles of a pruning shears sticking out of her pocket, scuffed sandals. She was holding an asparagus fern she had probably just brought in from the sidewalk outside; it was past closing time. She turned to look at me. Behind her was a display-cooler riotously packed with red long-stemmed roses and bright purple tulips, baby's breath and orchids, marguerite daisies and irises that echoed again the words LE FLEUR DE LIS elongated at the woman's feet in sunlit silhouette on the floor of the shop. To her left and right on shelves and hanging from the ceiling were kangaroo vines and snakeskin plants, cactus and Boston ivy, spider plants, flame violets, angel-wing begonias. A calico-cat flowerpot stood empty beside an arrangement of dried flowers.

"Excuse me," I said. "I'm looking for Mrs. Brenet."

"I'm Mrs. Brenet," she said. The blonde eyebrows arched a trifle, the brown eyes widened expectantly in the plump face.

"Catherine Brenet?" I said. I could not believe this was the woman Jamie had described as "startlingly beautiful."

"Yes," she said, "I'm Catherine Brenet."

"How do you do?" I said. "I'm Matthew Hope." I paused. "Jamie Purchase's attorney."

'Yes?" she said. She put down the asparagus fern, and made a small puzzled gesture with head and hands.

"I'd like to ask you some questions about last night," I said.

"I beg your pardon?" The look of bewilderment was turning to something else.

"Mrs. Brenet, I'm Jamie's attorney. I'm sure you know what happened last night—"

"Yes?" Again the single word as a question. But the

eyebrows were no longer arched. They were puckering into a frown above the thick-rimmed glasses.

"Jamie says he was with you last night between—"

"With me?" she said.

"Yes, between eleven and—"

"*Me?* Are you sure you've got the right person?"

"You *are* Catherine Brenet?"

"Yes."

"And you *do* know Jamie Purchase?"

"Yes. But I don't know what you mean about last night."

"His wife and children were—"

"Yes, I heard that on the radio. But when you say Dr. Purchase—"

"Mrs. Brenet, he told us that—"

"Was *with* me—"

"Between eleven and—"

"I don't understand."

We both stopped talking at the same time. She looked at me, waiting for an explanation. I looked at her, waiting for the same thing.

"Mr. Hope," she said at last, "my husband and I knew the Purchases only casually. I was, of course, distressed to learn of the terrible tragedy that had—"

"Mrs. Brenet, you're going to be visited shortly by a Detective Ehrenberg of the Calusa Pol—"

"What on earth for?"

"Because Jamie Purchase says he was with you last night between the hours of eleven and twelve-thirty."

"He wasn't."

"You didn't see him last night?"

"I haven't seen him since . . . I can't even remember. I believe I met him and his wife at a charity ball, oh, more than a year ago. And I think we saw each other once after that, at a dinner party someplace."

"Jamie said—"

"I don't care what—"

"He said you've been lovers for—"

"Don't be ridiculous."

"I'm repeating what he told us this morning."

"Told *who?*"

"My partner and me. In our offices this morning."

"Well, he was obviously . . . I can't imagine why he said anything like that. I don't know whether to be offended or flattered. I'm hardly the type of woman—"

"Mrs. Brenet, if Jamie wasn't with you last night, then he was somewhere else. And the police will want to know where."

"I'm sure that's *his* problem, not mine."

"I don't think you understand me."

"I understand you completely. You're asking me to provide an alibi for Dr. Purchase."

"I'm asking you to verify his story."

"How can I possibly do that?"

"Mrs. Brenet, Jamie told us that you and he have been renting a cottage on Whisper . . ."

"This is really too ridiculous."

"That you'd decided to seek divorces . . ."

"I'm a happily married woman. I would no more consider divorcing my husband than . . . I simply would never con*sid*er it."

"Then Jamie was lying."

"If he said he was with me last night, why yes. Of *course* he was lying."

"Where *were* you last night, Mrs. Brenet?"

"I don't think that's any of your business." She looked up at the wall clock. "I was just closing the shop when you got here. My husband and I have a dinner date, so if you don't mind—"

"Was your husband home last night?"

"Again, that's none of—"

"Are you asking me to believe that Jamie picked your name out of the air? Made up a long story about you on the spur of the moment—"

"I don't know why he told you what he did. If, indeed, he told you anything at all."

"He did."

"I'll accept your word for that. In which case, all I can say—again, and for the last time—is that he was lying."

"Will you tell that to the police when they get here?"

"What have *you* told them, Mr. Hope?"

"Nothing. They found out about you on their own."

"There was nothing to find out, so I can't imagine—"

"They talked to one of Jamie's nurses this afternoon. They know all about your frequent phone calls to his office."

"I'm sure I'm being confused with someone else."

"I don't think so."

"When the police get here, *if* they get here, I'll tell them I went to a movie last night. My husband, as it happens, was in Tampa visiting his mother—he goes to see her two or three times a month. She doesn't particularly like me, we try to avoid each other. When I got back to the house, my husband was already home. I asked him how his mother was. He said she was fine. We both went to sleep."

"Is that what you told your husband? That you'd gone to a movie?"

"I generally go to a movie when he's in Tampa with his mother. He stays with her most of the day and doesn't get home till quite late. There's nothing unusual about my having gone to a movie."

"So let me understand this . . ."

"I'm terribly pressed for—"

"Even if Jamie's in danger—"

"Really, Mr. Hope—"

"You won't admit he was with you last night. Because such an admission—"

"Mr. Hope, I read in this afternoon's *News* that his son has already confessed to the murders. Is that true?"

"It's true."

"Then good day, Mr. Hope."

So there we were.

There was Jamie Purchase's "startlingly beautiful" mistress, who had worn a black raincoat and a green hat that first day they met secretly. There had been rain in Calusa, so unusual for February. He had put his hand on her thigh the moment she'd entered the car, "the touch was electric," he'd told us. There had been the aroma of wet and steamy garments in that small contained space, the windshield wipers had snicked at the rain, snick, snick, snick—ah, *l'amour*. And ah, how that love had blossomed over the space of a year and a little bit more, till last night in a cottage by the sea, they had both sworn fealty, fealty forever, and had discussed the imminent demise of their respective mates—yes, that was the word Jamie had used. Mates. Not demise, oh no. The demise, presumably, was metaphoric, they had only talked of *leaving* their spouses. The waves had crashed in cinematically against the shore, *Soon, my darling, soon,* Burt and Deborah, Kim and Kirk, Elizabeth and Richard, and now, for the first time together in embrace on a beach, spume flying, J*A*M*I*E and C*A*T*H*E*R*I*N*E, he kisses her face, he kisses her throat, he kisses her eyes—I wanted to vomit.

A memorable moment, to be sure. So memorable that the dumpy little lady in the green smock seemed to have forgotten it completely less than seventeen hours later. Give her twenty-four and she'd forget her own name. But for now, at five-fifteen on a lovely Calusa afternoon, it was enough to have forgotten Jamie Purchase. Because remembering him would be endangering her marriage. Catherine was simply protecting her turf, that was all. She may have sworn to the stars and the sea that together she and Jamie would wend their way down life's thorny path; she may even have meant it. But the chips were down now, as surely as they'd been down in that poker game Jamie had tried to lose and could only succeed in winning. Her hand was being called. She could declare the pair of deuces or bluff a royal flush.

Jamie was safe, she thought. His son had confessed to the crime, there was no way Jamie could become involved, even if she denied having been with him last night. So Catherine was taking the odds on today, never mind the long shot on eternity; eternity was for graveyards. Catherine was opting for the good life she had with the surgeon; love and marriage, so to speak, house and garden, seashells arranged in an orderly row on a Lucite shelf, another charity ball next year, and the year after that, and the year after that after that. If she and Jamie ever got past this one—and she had to admit it looked a bit dicey just now—they might be able to pick up right where they'd left off before all the unpleasantness, same old stand next Wednesday or next Sunday, business as usual.

I suddenly wondered what Aggie would do in a similar situation.

Worse, I wondered what I myself would do.

There was a metallic taste in my mouth when I left the flower shop. As I drove away from the curb, Catherine Brenet was putting in the last of her plants, a heavy weeping fig that she struggled to carry to the open door of the shop.

10

I HEARD the burglar-alarm siren the moment I turned the corner into my street. I immediately looked at the dashboard clock. The timc was twenty-five minutes past five. I could not imagine why the siren was going, or why Reginald Soames was standing on the sidewalk in front of my house, together with a handful of other neighbors. The sound of the siren was piercing. I pulled into my driveway, got out of the car, and immediately said, "What is it? Has someone broken in?"

"Police have already been here," Reggie shouted. "Couldn't turn the damn thing off."

"Were the key holders here?"

"The *what?*"

"The key holders. There's two of them. If the alarm goes off—"

"Couldn't *turn* it off!" Reggie shouted.

"The key holders?"

"The *police.*"

"Did someone try to break in?"

"Your daughter hit the panic button."

"What? My daughter—"

"The *cat* got run over."

"Sebastian?"

"Run over by a car. Your daughter hit the panic button, figured that'd bring the police."

"Where's my wife?"

"Don't know where she is. Mrs. Tannenbaum drove your daughter and the cat to the vet's. Police were mad as hell. Been trying to get you at the office, Junior, you shouldn't be out sailing on a workday."

"What vet did they take him to, do you know?"

"Haven't the faintest. You'd better turn that siren off, Mr. Ziprodt up the block's got a bad heart."

The front door was unlocked. I went directly through the house and to the back door, where one of the alarm stations was set into the wall just outside. I took my key ring from my pocket, and searched for the key to the system, wishing it were color-coded like the key at the jail. The siren was still screaming. I found the right key at last, put it in the keyway, and turned it to the right. The siren stopped abruptly. The silence was almost deafening. I went back into the house and to the utility closet, where the burglar alarm control box was mounted on the wall alongside a circuit breaker. I opened the front panel of the box and reset the system, but not the alarm; this had to be done whenever the panic button was hit. I slammed the panel shut, and went immediately to the phone in the study. In the yellow pages, I found under VETERINARIANS-D.V.M. at least a dozen listings. I scanned them quickly, found one that sounded familiar, dialed the number, and asked for Dr. Roessler.

"Dr. Roessler is in surgery, sir."

"Who's this I'm speaking to, please?"

"Miss Hilmer."

"Miss Hilmer, this is Matthew Hope, I'm calling about a gray tabby named Sebastian. Would you—"

"Yes, sir, the cat's here."

"How is he?"

"He's being operated on now, sir."

"Can you tell me what . . . how bad is it?"

"His thorax is torn, Mr. Hope. The lungs and heart are exposed. Dr. Roessler is closing the wound now."

"Thank you, could I . . . is my daughter there?"

"Just a moment, sir."

When Joanna got on the line, I said, "Honey, I'm on my way, you just wait there for me."

"Dad," she said, "I think he's going to die."

"Well, we don't know that, honey."

"I tried calling, where were you?"

"With a client."

"Cynthia said you were on a boat."

"Yes, I went there first to talk to someone, and then I went to the police department to talk to Michael Purchase."

"I heard on the radio that Michael did it, is that true?"

"I don't know. Honey, is Mrs. Tannenbaum still there with you?"

"Yes. Did you want to talk to her?"

"No, that's all right. But please ask her to stay till I get there, would you? Where's Mommy?"

"I think she went to the beauty parlor, I'm not sure."

"All right, honey, I'll see you in a few minutes."

"Do you know how to get here?"

"It's near Cross River, isn't it?"

"Yes."

"I'll remember it when I see it. G'bye, darling."

"Bye, Dad," she said, and hung up.

All the way to the vet's, I kept thinking of Sebastian.

On the day before we'd taken him into the family, Susan had gone down to the basement of our house in Chicago, and found herself face to face with a rat the size of an alligator. Brazen bastard got up on his hind legs and snarled and squealed, sent her screaming up out of the cellar to phone an exterminator who came that afternoon to seed the basement floor with poison pellets. Trouble was, we had a five-year-old daughter and I didn't like the idea of all that poison lying around, however infrequently she might be visiting the basement. Susan began crying when I suggested the possible danger to Joanna, immediately thinking I was scolding her for having called the exterminator. I told her she'd done exactly the right thing, but that a cat might be a safer deterrent than scattered poison patties.

What I had in mind was a *big* cat.

I suppose the range of animals varies at any given shelter on any given day. On that particular day in March, seven years ago, there were two cats, eleven kittens, five mongrel dogs, and the most beautiful thoroughbred boxer I'd ever seen. Sebastian was one of the cats, an enormous gray tabby with darker gray stripes, white markings on his face, markings that looked like white socks on all four paws. The one on his right hind paw seemed to have slipped to his ankle. He was prowling the topmost shelf of a cage that contained two separate litters of kittens and a scrawny Siamese that was not only cross-eyed but looked mangy as well. Sebastian paced the shelf like a tiger. He looked fierce and proud and I was certain he was the best rat-catcher who'd ever stalked a basement. "Hey, there," I said, and he looked at me with the greenest eyes I'd ever seen on man or beast, and gave a short "meow," and I fell in love with that big old pussycat right then and there. Susan had wandered down to the other end of the room, where she was looking at the boxer. I called her over.

"Well, he's certainly big enough," she said.

"Look at those green eyes, Sue."

"Mm," she said.

"Let's find out why he's here. Maybe he ate his former owners."

We went outside to where a young man was filling out papers behind a desk. I asked him about the big gray tabby. Was there anything wrong with him?

"No, the mother was allergic to him," he said.

"The cat's mother?"

"No, the mother in the family. He's the gentlest cat. Not a thing wrong with him."

"What's his name?"

"Sabbatical."

"What?"

"Yeah, she's a schoolteacher. The mother."

"That's no name," I said.

"Well, that's *his* name."

Susan and I went back inside again. The cat was still

up there on the top shelf, licking himself clean now. We stood outside the cage, watching him.

"What do you think?" I said.

"Well, I don't know," Susan said. "I was hoping we'd find a *white* cat."

"Is he huge, or am I dreaming?"

"He's enormous."

"Hey, Sebastian," I said, and the cat meowed again.

Ten minutes later, we were taking him home in a cardboard carrier. We'd given a donation of twenty-five dollars to the shelter, and already had misgivings about this unknown cat without papers or pedigree. Sebastian broke out of the carrier before we'd driven five miles from the shelter. First his ears popped up out of the opening, then his green eyes wide and curious, and at last his face, white mask over the nose and mouth. He climbed out onto the back seat and looked around.

"The cat's out," Susan said.

"Oh, shit," I said.

But Sebastian only leaped up onto the little ledge inside the rear window, and sprawled there to watch the scenery going by. Never made a sound, didn't scramble all over the place like most lunatic cats do in a moving automobile. Just sat there with those big green eyes taking in everything. Automobiles never frightened him. One morning—this was after we'd been living in Calusa for almost a year—I got into the Ghia and had driven halfway to the office when I heard a sound behind me. I turned to look, and there was Sebastian sitting on the back seat. I grinned and said, "Hey, Sebastian, what are you doing there, huh?" He blinked. Joanna played with him as if he were a puppy. Hide-and-seek, games with string or yarn, races across the lawn. One time she came into the bedroom, beaming, to describe a game she and Sebastian had been playing. "We had the *most* fun," she said. "I was chasing him around the sofa, and he was laughing and laughing." She really did believe he was laughing. I guess I believed it, too. For some reason, perhaps because we'd got him close to St. Patrick's Day, we all thought of Sebastian as Irish. I'd sometimes talk to him in a thick Irish brogue, and he'd roll over on his back to reveal the whitest, softest, furriest belly, and I'd tickle him—and yes, he was laughing, I'm sure he was laughing.

I loved that cat with all my heart.

The veterinary hospital was set on a street with three used-car lots and a store selling model airplanes. I parked the Ghia alongside a Chevy station wagon I recognized as Mrs. Tannenbaum's, and then began walking across the parking lot toward the front door. From the kennel behind the red brick building, I heard a chorus of barks and yelps. My immediate reaction was to wonder what all that canine clamor might be doing to Sebastian's nerves. And then I realized he was no doubt still unconscious, and my step slowed as I came closer to the door. I did not want to open that door. I was afraid that once I stepped inside, someone would tell me Sebastian was dead.

There was a desk immediately facing the entrance door. A nurse in a starched white uniform sat behind it; she looked up as I came into the room. Joanna and Mrs. Tannenbaum were sitting on a bench against the wall on the left. A framed painting of a cocker spaniel was on the wall above their heads. I went immediately to my daughter, and sat beside her, and put my arm around her.

"How is he?" I asked.

"They're still working on him."

We were whispering.

I leaned over and said, "Mrs. Tannenbaum, I can't thank you enough."

"I'm glad I could help," she said. Her first name was Gertrude. I'd never called her that. She was seventy-two years old, but she looked sixty, and knew more about boats than any man I'd ever met. Her husband had died ten years back, leaving her a twin-dieseled Matthews Mystic she did not know how to operate. She enrolled promptly in the Auxiliary Coast Guard's boating safety course, and a year later took that boat from Calusa past Charlotte Harbor, into the Caloosahatchee River and then into Lake Okeechobee and the St. Lucie Canal, across the state to Stuart and Lake Worth, where she'd jumped off across the

Gulf Stream for Bimini. She had lavender hair and blue eyes and she was tiny and wiry, but when she wrestled that forty-six-footer into a dock you'd think she was on the bridge of an aircraft carrier.

"Tell me what happened," I said.

"I got home from school about three-thirty," Joanna said, "and I looked for Sebastian, but he wasn't anywhere around. I was going to the mailbox to see if there was anything for me, and I just happened to look across the street—do you know where that big gold tree is on Dr. Latty's lawn? Right there, near the curb. Sebastian was . . . he was just lying there in the gutter. I thought at first . . . I don't know what I thought. That he was . . . playing a game with me, I guess. And then I saw the blood . . . oh God, Dad. I didn't know what to do. I went over to him, I said, 'Sebastian? What . . . what's the matter, baby?' And his eyes . . . he looked up the way he sometimes does when he's napping, you know, and he still has that drowsy look on his face . . . only . . . oh Dad, he looked so . . . so twisted and broken, I didn't . . . I just didn't know what to do to help him. So I came back in the house and called your office but they told me you were out on a boat—what were you doing on a boat, Dad?"

"Talking to Michael's girlfriend," I said, which was true enough. But by three-thirty, I had left the boat and was in bed with Aggie. I thought again of Jamie's alibi for last night. Would his wife and children have been slain if he'd gone directly home at eleven, rather than to the beach cottage he shared with the surgeon's wife? And similarly, would I have been able to help Sebastian if I'd been at my office when Joanna called?

"I didn't know what to do," she said. "I didn't know where Mom was, and I couldn't get in touch with you, so I just went in the bedroom and hit the panic button. I figured that'd bring everybody running. Mr. Soames from next door came over, and then Mrs. Tannenbaum—"

"I heard the siren, I thought at first it was some crazies come to rob your house in broad daylight. It could happen, believe me."

"She drove the wagon to where Sebastian was against the curb—"

"We picked him up very careful. We made a stretcher from a board I had in the garage. We lifted him only a little, enough to get him on the board."

"Then we came right here. I knew where it was from when he had his shots last time."

"What did Dr. Roessler say?"

"Daddy, he doesn't think Sebastian's going to live."

"He said that?"

"Yes, Dad."

There seemed nothing more to say. I told Mrs. Tannenbaum I was sure she wanted to get home, and I thanked her again, and she asked me to please call her as soon as we got back. We sat alone on the bench then, my daughter and I. I held her hand. Across the room, the nurse was busily inserting what I supposed to be bills into envelopes. To her right was a closed door. To the left of that was an aquarium with tropical fish in it. Air bubbles tirelessly climbed the inside of the tank.

The last time I'd been inside a hospital was two years ago, when Susan's mother died. She was fifty-six years old, and had never smoked a cigarette in her lifetime; but both her lungs were riddled with cancer. They'd performed the biopsy, and then closed her up, and told us there was nothing they could do for her. It was Susan's uncle who made the decision not to tell her she was dying. I'd disliked him before then, but that was when I began hating him. She was, you see, a marvelous woman who could have accepted the news, who would in fact have welcomed the opportunity to die with at least some measure of dignity. Instead . . . ah, Jesus.

I remembered going to the hospital one afternoon, I went alone, I don't remember where Susan was. I think she simply had to get away from the vigil for just a little bit, it was taking so much out of her. I went there, and my mother-in-law was propped against the pillows, her head turned to one side, where sunlight was coming through the slatted venetian blinds. She had Susan's features and coloring exactly, the same dark eyes and chestnut hair, the full pouting mouth showing age wrinkles around its edges now, the good jaw and neck, the skin sagging somewhat—she'd been a beauty in her day, and she looked beautiful still though ravaged with disease, and rapidly dying. She was weeping when I came into the room. I sat beside the bed. I said, "Mom, what's the matter? What is it?"

She took my hand between both hers. Tears were streaming down her face. She said, "Matthew, please tell them I'm trying."

"Tell who, Mom?"

"The doctors."

"What do you mean?"

"They think I'm not trying. I really am, I really do want to get better. I just haven't got the strength, Matthew."

"I'll talk to them," I said.

I found one of her doctors in the corridor later that day. I asked him what he'd told her. He said it had been the family's decision—

"I'm the goddamn family, too," I said. "What did you tell her?"

"I was merely trying to reassure her, Mr. Hope."

"About what?"

"I told her she would get well. That if she tried hard enough—"

"That's a lie."

"It was the family's decision—"

"No matter *how* hard she tries, she's going to die."

"Mr. Hope, really, I feel you should discuss this with your wife's uncle. I was trying to help her maintain her spirit, that's all," the doctor said, and turned on his heel and walked off down the corridor. My mother-in-law died the following week. She never knew she was dying. I suspected it came as a total surprise to her when she drew her last breath. I kept thinking of her that way; as dying in surprise. I loved her a lot, that woman. I think she was one of the reasons I married Susan.

I sat now beside my daughter, and wondered if I could ever tell Aggie how I'd felt about my mother-in-law. Wondered if I could ever tell her about Sebastian getting hit by an automobile, and about *this* family vigil at *this* hospital, where another loved one was fighting for life. Would it mean anything to Aggie? Would the death of Sebastian, whom she had never seen and did not know, mean anything more to her than the death of my mother-in-law? I realized all at once that I was already thinking of Sebastian as dead. I squeezed my daughter's hand. I remembered coming home from Chicago, after we'd buried Susan's mother. Joanna was waiting at the door with her sitter. We had not told her on the telephone that her grandmother was dead. She asked immediately, "How's Grandma?"

"Honey . . ." I said, and did not have to say another word.

Joanna covered her face with her hands, and ran to her room in tears.

There was a computerized memory-bank we'd shared together for the past thirteen years, Susan and I. Into it we had programmed a mutual set of experiences that could be recalled at the touch of a button or the flip of a switch. Susan's mother was a part of what we had known together, and loved together. I wondered now what would happen when at last I mustered the courage—yes, courage—to tell Susan I wanted a divorce. Would I be able to get past the first word "Honey" before she, too, burst into tears? It was funny how the word lingered, how we continued using it as a term of endearment, even though it had long ago lost any real meaning, at least for me. But it had been fed into the computer—HONEY, EXPRESSION OF AFFECTION, SUSAN/MATTHEW—and there was no changing the data now, except through direct confrontation. *Susan, I want a divorce.* Click, whir, the tapes would spin, the new information would be recorded and replayed. SCRATCH SUSAN/WIFE, SUBSTITUTE AGGIE/WIFE. But when that happened, would I have to change the memory-bank as well? Would I have to pretend I'd never been in that hospital room with my mother-in-law weeping helplessly against her pillows, my hand clutched between her own? Would I have to *forget* her?

Sitting on that wooden bench, watching the bubbles rise in the fish tank, expecting to hear momentarily that Sebastian was dead, I wondered what my mother-in-law would say if she were still alive and I came to her with news that I was divorcing Susan. I thought perhaps she would listen with the same dignity she might have given news that she was dying. And afterward, she might take my hand between her own two hands as she'd done that day at the hospital, and look directly into my eyes in that level, honest way she had—Jesus, how I'd loved that woman! Susan used to have the same direct way of looking at me. It had vanished somewhere, perhaps to wherever it was that Susan herself had gone.

Her mother would want to know why. She would hold my hands and say But, Matthew . . . why? And I would say Mom, we haven't got along now for the past five years, we thought the move to Florida might help, we thought there was something about Illinois . . . my job there, the people we knew there . . . that was causing us to drift apart. But we've been living here for three years now and nothing's changed, except that it's getting worse all the time, a day doesn't go by that we aren't fighting . . .

Mom, I'm not happy.

I don't love her.

We're neither of us the same people we married almost fourteen years ago; it seems ridiculous now that we ever thought we'd stay the same. We should have hoped instead that the person each of us eventually became would be someone we could still love. I can't love her anymore. Jesus, I've *tried*. So what can I do, Mom? What else can I do but leave her? And my mother-in-law, if she were still alive, might say Matthew, do what you have to do. Maybe she'd say that. And then maybe she'd ask me if there was another woman, yes, I was certain she'd ask that. And when I told her there was, she might want to know about her, might ask . . . no, I didn't think so.

As I sat beside my daughter waiting for word about Sebastian, I realize the relationship would end right then and there; I would be divorcing Susan's mother together with Susan. I was suddenly grateful that I'd never have to face her, never have to tell her I was moving out of her life. But the relief I felt was out of all proportion to the reality of the situation—my mother-in-law was dead, there wasn't the faintest possibility I'd ever have to tell her I was divorcing her daughter. And I realized then that it was *Susan* I didn't want to tell, *Susan* I was reluctant to confront, perhaps even ashamed to confront. Did I simply go to her now and say, "Honey . . ." I would choke on the first word, knowing for sure that I was about to short-circuit the computer forever, wipe the tape entirely clean, program it with new people and new experiences that only with time might become memories to recall.

The thought was frightening.

I did not want to push the MOTHER-IN-LAW button one day and conjure Aggie's mother who lived in Cambridge, Massachusetts, and whom I'd not yet met. No. I wanted to recall Susan's mother, who'd held my hand in hers and told me she was trying. When I pressed the DAUGHTER button, I did not want the daughter of Gerald Hemmings to appear, *his* daughter, I did not want to see baby pictures of Julia Hemmings, I did not want *their* memory-bank to become *mine*. When I pushed DAUGHTER, I wanted Joanna to fill the screen of my mind in full color, twenty times larger than life, Joanna smiling, Joanna shoveling soggy cornflakes into her mouth, Joanna falling and splitting her lip when she was three, Joanna, my daughter.

And when I pressed the button that had PET printed on it in bright green for Sebastian's eyes, I did not want Julia's goldfish to appear, which I'd seen in Julia's room, the room of a little girl I had not yet met, the room of a little girl who was *not* my daughter but who would *become* my daughter, my stepdaughter, my whatever-the-hell the moment I changed the computer, the moment I fed into it all this new data—no! When I pushed the PET button, I wanted to see Sebastian's big masked face and those emerald Irish eyes of his, I wanted to recall all the marvelous things about him, the way he stalked lizards as though they were dinosaurs, the way his ears twitched when he was listening to the Modern Jazz—

"Mr. Hope?"

I looked toward the open door. Dr. Roessler still had his hand on the doorknob. There was no need for him to say anything further. I knew the moment I saw his face that Sebastian the cat was dead.

He really hadn't had a chance.

Dr. Roessler had been forced to operate at once. In

order for Sebastian to begin breathing normally again, there had to be a vacuum between his lungs and his ribs; the torn thorax had to be sutured immediately. But there were other problems as well. A rib bone had been driven into one of his lungs and had punctured it. His pelvis was crushed. There was a huge rupture in his diaphragm, between the chest and abdomen. Dr. Roessler told us he would have preferred treating him first with massive doses of cortisone and I.V. fluid, hoping to stabilize his condition, waiting a full twenty-four hours before surgery. But there had been no choice; Sebastian was taken into the operating room the moment he was brought in.

Dr. Roessler apologized now. He said Sebastian was a fine cat, he remembered him from other times he'd been here. He said he had done his very best. His face was beaded with perspiration. There were flecks of blood on his gown. He said again that he was sorry, and then excused himself and left the small reception room. His nurse took me aside and asked what I would want to do with the body. She said there was a man who came by to pick up animals for burial, he carried them to Palmetto, he did a very good job. She said that some families preferred to have the animal cremated, but this was very costly. Most families took the body with them, she said, and buried the animal themselves. Most of them used a Styrofoam ice chest. I told her we wanted to take Sebastian with us. She went through the door and was gone just a little while. When she came back, she was carrying a heavy-duty black plastic bag weighted with Sebastian's body. She told me the bag was waterproof. I carried the bag out to the car and put it on the folded-down back seat. I could remember Sebastian sitting on that seat, alive, the morning I'd driven him halfway to work. "Hey, Sebastian, what are you doing there, huh?" Sebastian blinking.

We were silent for a long while, Joanna and I.

When at last we talked, it was not about Sebastian. Not at first.

My daughter told me she'd weighed herself that morning, and was three pounds overweight. She was getting fat again. She didn't know why, she'd been watching her diet very carefully. I told her she wasn't getting fat at all. She was a tall girl, she was still growing . . .

"Really, darling, you're not getting fat. I'd tell you if you were."

"I'm not that tall," Joanna said. "Crystal is much taller than I am, and she weighs six pounds less than I do."

"Crystal is skinny."

"Dad, she has a beautiful figure."

"She's skinny."

"She has breasts, and I don't."

"You'll have breasts soon enough, don't worry about it."

"And this rash around my nose, Dad, we went to the dermatologist and he doesn't know what it is, he just keeps telling me to wash my damn face three times a day. Well, I *do* wash my face, I wash it four, *five* times a day, and I've still got all this junk around my nose, I look terrible, Dad. If it doesn't go away soon, can Mom take me to another doctor?"

"Yes, darling."

"Because it isn't acne, he admits it isn't acne."

"We'll get rid of it, darling, don't worry."

"Dad . . ."

"Yes, sweetheart?"

"He was like a person, you know? Sebastian. He was just like a person."

We buried him in the back yard.

There was a spot under the poinciana tree, where Sebastian used to lie flat to watch the pelicans swooping in low over the water, his ears twitching, his tail snapping back and forth like a whip. We buried him there. It was twenty-five past six, and beginning to get dark. Susan was not home yet. I found myself getting angry at her for not being here when Joanna found the cat broken and hurt in the gutter, for not being here now when we were burying him.

I asked Joanna if there was anything she wanted to say.

She knelt by the open grave and placed a small orange seashell onto the Styrofoam chest we'd bought on the way home. "I love you, Sebastian," she said, and that was all.

I shoveled back sand and then topsoil, and replaced the rectangle of grass I'd earlier carefully removed. Joanna put her arm around my waist. Silently, we went back into the house together. I poured myself a stiff hooker of Scotch over ice, and asked Joanna if she wanted a beer. She nodded. I opened a can and handed it to her. She took a sip and said, "I hate the taste of beer," but she kept drinking it, anyway.

Susan stormed into the house ten minutes later.

She'd come out of her hairdresser's to find the right front tire of her Mercedes flat. She'd called our local gas station for help, but it had taken them an hour to get there, and another twenty minutes to put on the spare. Then, on the way home, the causeway bridge got stuck open for another—

"Is that *beer* you're drinking, Joanna?"

"Yes, Mom," Joanna said.

"Did you give her *beer* to drink?" Susan said, whirling on me.

"Yes, I gave her beer to drink. Susan . . . the cat's dead. Sebastian's dead."

"What?"

"He got hit by a car, honey."

"Oh," Susan said, and put her hand to her mouth. "Oh," she said, "oh," and began weeping, surprising me.

11

THE PARTY was being held on the twelfth floor of an oceanfront condominium on Stone Crab. The moment we stepped off the elevator, we were greeted by the sound of music and laughter coming from beyond the open door to the apartment on the left. Inside the apartment, some fifty or more people milled about against an extraordinary backdrop of sky and sea; the entire western wall of the apartment was open to the Gulf of Mexico. Lights on the beach below illuminated an irregular white curving line where the surf broke. The sky above was black, sprinkled with stars, hung with a full moon shimmering in a halo. On the wall opposite the windows, running the entire length of the room and broken only by a pair of open arches at either end, was a wall alive with a magnificent collection of paintings.

The guest of honor was a painter himself, an Italian whose show had opened earlier in the evening at a downtown gallery. His host and hostess had been collecting his work for years, and had invited us to the gallery opening as well as to this private party following it. But the invitation to the opening had read 5:00 to 7:00 P.M., and Susan hadn't come home till a quarter to; there was no way we could possibly have got there on time. I suggested that we skip the party, too, but Susan wisely offered the advice that it would do no good to mope around waiting for Sebastian to come padding around every corner of the house.

As we made our way toward the bar set up just past the distant arch, I heard a woman mention Emily Purchase's name, heard her telling another woman that her daughter was in the same first-grade class at school. At the bar, two men were talking about the confession Michael Purchase had made. It seemed that while Joanna and I were out burying Sebastian, the State's Attorney was making a brief television appearance on the six o'clock news, reiterating much of what had already been printed in the afternoon paper. He told the assembled reporters that Michael Allen Purchase, the twenty-year-old son of the man whose wife and daughters had been slain, was being held for first-degree murder on an arrest warrant issued by a circuit judge. Detective Ehrenberg, the police officer conducting the investigation, had obtained a confession from the youth—one of the men at the bar now demanded to know from the other why the State's Attorney referred to a twenty-year-old *man* as a *youth!*—and when the grand jury was called to render a decision on the facts of the case, hopefully by Friday at the latest, the State's Attorney was certain they would indict for first-degree murder. When asked by one of the reporters whether the murder weapon had yet been found, he replied at once, "The boy threw the knife in the Gulf, from what I understand."

"Did he say why he killed them?" another reporter asked.

"I'm afraid I can't comment on that at this time."

"Is rape a consideration in this case, sir?"

"No comment."

"Does that mean yes?"

"It means no comment."

I turned away from the bar. Susan was already moving into the crowd, drink in hand, toward where Leona and Frank were standing near the buffet table. Leona was wearing a black pants suit, the jacket of which was slashed to her navel. Frank referred to her somewhat exuberant breasts as "the family jewels," and maintained that Leona's penchant for wearing revealing garments at every Calusa social event was akin to tossing "pearls before swine." Frank himself was wearing a brightly colored long-sleeved sports shirt, and what I recognized at once as his Italian pants. He had bought them in Milan two years ago, and wore them so often that I once accused him of having only two pair of pants—the ones he wore to the office with a ratty sports jacket, and the Italian pair he wore to parties. The Italian pair had only one pocket, on the right hip. As a result, Frank wore a little leather purse, which he'd also bought in Milan, attached to his belt. I signaled to him, and started across the room. Susan had already reached them. She was hugging Leona now, kissing Frank on the cheek at the same time.

Someone stopped me, a man I'd met casually at another party, I couldn't remember his name. He asked if I knew I'd been mentioned on television tonight in connection with the Purchase murder case. Said one of the reporters asked who the boy's lawyer was, and the State's Attorney said he believed it was Matthew Hope. He began giving me his own ideas on the case then, constantly referring to it as The Purchase Murder Case, capitalizing it like the title of a novel or a film—T*H*E P*U*R*C*H*A*S*E M*U*R-D*E*R C*A*S*E—and I realized all at once that he was treating it like a suspense story, which it certainly was not. Not to the victims. Not to Jamie or his son. Not even to me. But to this man, the tragedy was only a murder mystery, and he recounted it to me as such now, reducing it to the level of a whodunit.

This is the cast of characters: a father, a son, a stepmother and two half sisters. This is the plot: the father comes home from a poker game to find his wife and daughters slain. The son later confesses to the crime. Open and shut, the State's Attorney says. Next case, the judge says. But, ah, that wasn't enough. The man who had hold of my elbow and my ear, the man sipping champagne here from a stemmed plastic glass, needed something more. I could not imagine what essential ingredient was missing. Perhaps he only wanted another body to float up from the bayou behind Jamie's house, which the State's Attorney had mentioned by name, I was now informed, and which name—Fairy Bayou—caused my unknown friend here to comment that it was undoubtedly named after a closet queen up the street. He guffawed at this, and I seized the opportunity to drift away from him on the crest of my own mirthless laughter.

The talk everywhere around me was of the murders on Jacaranda. Lacking another body, or another spate of bodies, lacking even another suspect—no butler to cast long menacing looks, no lady in a black raincoat running for the misty heath, no crazy old uncle in the tower room babbling about what he'd seen—why then the obvious questions had to be asked about the facts that existed. And the people here at the party seemed to find the facts questionable at best. I heard someone ask whether Jamie Purchase was really at a poker game the night before, as had been mentioned in the newspapers, though not in the State's Attorney's interview. Or had he possibly *left* the poker game early, and gone back home to kill his own wife and children? This particular cynic, of course, did not know that Jamie had indeed left the poker game early, or that he'd gone not home but to the bed of his loving surgeon's wife. Or so Jamie claimed, an alibi that Catherine Brenet had already effectively demolished, dear loyal Kate. The Calusans gathered here to honor the Italian painter knew nothing of Jamie's love life, however, and so they *guessed* he might have been somewhere else, the parlor game of murder becoming pallid if one could not speculate on intrigue and romance, poison rings and stilettos.

Which brought the partygoers to the matter of the murder weapon itself, the very same weapon the State's Attorney had described on television as having been thrown in the Gulf. Well, no one here expected the police to drag an ocean in search of a bread knife, or *whatever* kind of knife it was—the newspapers simply described the murder weapon as "a big kitchen knife," information presumably given to them by the Police Department, or the State's Attorney's office, or both. But it seemed to almost everyone present, judging from what I could overhear, that a knife of that size and weight, even if it sank to the bottom when it was first thrown in the water, would by this time have been washed ashore, the tide having come in—as one expert sport fisherman was quick to ascertain—at 12:59 P.M. this afternoon.

I heard the Italian artist telling someone in broken English, that he had been flown from Naples, Italy, to Rome and then New York and Miami, and had been driven there to Naples, Florida, because the big promotional idea was "*Da Napoli a Napoli, from* Nepples *to* Nepples, you unnerstan?" But the gallery opening there had been a huge disappointment, largely due to the fact that his work was far too young and vigorous for the Florida Neopolitans—"*gli anziani,*" he called them. So he'd come up here to Calusa, there had been a nice crowd at the show tonight, nice-dressed people, plenty money, and what did they talk about? They talked about murder! His host assured him that this was an unusual circumstance, there were hardly *ever* any murders in Calusa. The Italian rolled his eyes and said, "*Allora, perche me?* Why he dinna wait some *other* time?"

Susan looked spectacular.

She was wearing a white silk jersey tunic, belted at the waist with a golden rope and draped over a long white matching skirt. Gold sandals and gold hoop earrings, a hammered-gold cuff-bracelet on her right wrist. Her hair was pulled tightly to the back of her head, held there with a golden comb. She looked altogether sleek and sinuous, somewhat Grecian, her mouth slightly pouting as always, that spoiled sullen cast to her face, the brown eyes challenging falsely.

The glances she flashed about the room were only distant relatives of what had been her mother's direct and honest look. Susan took the legacy and wasted it. The look became calculated, she used it to foster an aura of anticipation, a breathlessness accompanying the direct eye contact. She flirted outrageously, my darling wife, and later denied it, outraged. Over Leona's shoulder, she met the Italian painter's eyes now, and when his own eyes sparked with interest, she cut him dead with a sudden lowering of long lashes and a faint superior smile. The first time I'd seen her years ago I especially wanted to take her to bed because she looked so damn superior. I wanted her to groan beneath me. I wanted her to whisper gutter talk in my ear. She could still excite me, I realized. She was wearing no bra, her gown clung to her breasts; as I approached her I actually found myself trying to peek into its low-cut front.

I shook hands with Frank, and a pair of cross-conversations immediately developed, Frank filling me in on what had happened at the office after I left today, Susan telling Leona about Sebastian's accident. True, most everything she said or did managed to annoy me lately, but this annoyed me particularly. It seemed to me that she was using the death of the cat to solicit sympathy and solace or—even more unforgivable—to call attention to herself as someone grieving and bereft. So I listened partially to what Frank was saying, and partially to what Susan was saying, and I heard Leona's clucking little sounds of condolence, and then somewhere on my left I heard a woman talking about the murders. It was the woman's question that captured my full attention.

She was asking the man at her side whether he thought Maureen and the two girls had been raped. I suspected she was deliberately leading the conversation into sexual channels, but the man missed his cue and responded with a long discourse on the sex offender in America, lacing it with statistics on how many homicides and aggravated assaults had been committed in conjunction with the crime of rape. Benny Fried, the criminal lawyer I'd tried to convince Michael to retain, once told me, "Matt, there *are* no mysteries. There are only crimes with motives for them." The one thing Michael Purchase did not seem to have was a motive. I tried to remember now what he had told me this afternoon. While the buzz of homicidal cocktail chatter swelled around me, while Frank told me about a visit from an Internal Revenue agent questioning the valuation of a decedent's estate, while Susan tried to explain the extent of the injuries that had caused Sebastian's death, I tried to reconstruct sentence by sentence the conversation I'd had with Michael. I could recall the gist and many of the details, but for the most part I could remember verbatim only snatches of what he'd said—and I had the certain feeling it was important to remember *exactly* what he'd said if I was to know *exactly* what had happened.

He'd told me that Maureen was the woman who'd called him, said she wanted to see him, asked him to come to the house. She'd referred to his sisters as the little girls, yes, I was sure that's what he'd said, the little girls were there, the three of them were there, Maureen and the little girls. But why had she given him this information? Was it to reassure him that she was alone except for the children? Had she further told him Emily and Eve were already asleep? Was she advising him the coast was clear?

She was scared.

Why?

Of . . . she didn't know what to do.

About what?

I don't know.

Michael Purchase had a way of not knowing, of not remembering. He could describe in detail the rosette on the low neck of a nightgown, but he could not recall why he had reached for a kitchen knife and chased his stepmother into the bedroom. Kissed her on the mouth. *I took her in my arms. I kissed her on the mouth.* Was he trying to tell me he'd raped her? Was this what he was conveniently forgetting—that he'd been *forced* to kill her because first he'd raped her? But he'd earlier told me he *hadn't* raped her, and he seemed genuinely shaken when he confessed to kissing her. *She was my father's wife, I'd kissed her.* He'd told Ehrenberg he'd only *hugged* her, though, so maybe he was leading up to the whole truth in gradual steps, I hugged her, I kissed her, I raped her, yes!

You kissed her after she was dead?

Yes.

In which case, and assuming kissing was a euphemism for something more sordid, Michael Purchase hadn't gone immediately to the police only because he knew what their reaction would be to necrophilia. Maybe he was *what* his father had called him this morning—a monster.

Did you kiss Emily, too?

No, just my mother.

Your mother?

Maureen.

There were darknesses here I no longer cared to explore. I closed my mind to what Michael had told me, closed it as well to the talk of murder everywhere around me. Our host was standing with the Italian artist, placating him, telling him the turnout at the gallery tonight had been truly remarkable.

Our hostess was calling us to dinner.

We got home at twenty to twelve. I checked on Joanna, who was sound asleep, and then went into the study to switch on the telephone-answering machine. The first message was from a client for whom I'd recently drawn a will. He said his son had been arrested driving a motorcycle at ninety miles an hour in a forty-mile zone. I made a note to call him in the morning, and then switched on the machine again. The next message was from Karin Purchase, leaving a phone number, and asking that I return her call. Jamie's daughter, according to what he'd told Ehrenberg, had been living in New York City for the past three years, but the number she'd left began with a 366—a Calusa prefix. I dialed it at once.

"Calusa Bay Hotel, good evening," a voice said. "May I help you?"

"Miss Karin Purchase, please," I said.

"Thank you, sir."

I waited. I could hear the phone ringing on the other end. I began counting the rings. I was about to hang up when a woman's voice said, "Hello?"

"Miss Purchase?"

"Yes?"

"Matthew Hope."

"Oh, hello, Mr. Hope, I was hoping you'd call, what time is it? I'm sorry, I was in the shower, where did I put my watch? A quarter to twelve, is that too late? I'd like to see you, do you think you can come here now, it's very important that we talk."

"Well . . ."

"It's room 401," she said, "can you get here in ten minutes or so, I'll be expecting you," she said, and hung up.

12

TALL, LISSOME, wearing a striped caftan slit at the neck, slit at the sides, blue eyes shadowed with a deeper blue, wet blonde hair captured in a scarf that matched the caftan, Karin Purchase opened the door and said at once, "Come in, you got here fast," slurring the sentences so that they became a single hurried invitation-observation. She turned and walked into the room. I followed her in, closing the door behind me.

She resembled her father strikingly, the same light blue eyes and arching blonde eyebrows, the same flaring nose and thin-lipped mouth. But there was in her angular length something entirely female as well. Slender arms showed in the kited sleeves of the caftan, collar bones veered wildly in the V-neck, narrow ankles and youthful legs flashed where the long skirt was slit to the knee on either side.

"Would you like a drink?" she asked. "Some Cognac? Creme de menthe?"

"Cognac, please," I said, and to my surprise she picked up the telephone receiver at once and asked for room service. It occurred to me belatedly that a young woman traveling alone, or for that matter a dowager traveling with an entourage, would not have packed her suitcase with a selection of after-dinner drinks. I felt like a clodhopper.

Karin Purchase's cool assurance was unsettling; she was far too young to be so smooth. How old had Jamie said? Twenty-two?

"This is Miss Purchase in 401," she said into the phone. "Would you please send up a cognac and a Grand Marnier?" She looked across at me. "Courvoisier all right?"

"Yes," I said.

"Courvoisier's fine, thank you," she said, and hung up, and immediately said, "I read about it in the *Post,* that's New York's afternoon paper, are you familiar with it? Said my brother had confessed to killing Maureen and the two girls." She shook her head, took a cigarette from a package on the dresser. Lighting it, she said, "There's a five-forty-five plane out of Newark." She blew out the match, exhaling a stream of smoke that looked like a visible sigh. "I got to the airport here at a little past ten, and called you the minute I was in the room."

"Why me?"

"The paper said you were representing Michael. Aren't you?"

"More or less."

"What does that mean, Mr. Hope?"

"It means your brother doesn't seem to want representation."

"I love my brother dearly, but he's a fool—"

"I've tried to indicate as much to him."

"He didn't commit those murders."

"He says he did. I was there when he made his statement to the police."

"I don't care what he told the police," Karin said. "I know otherwise."

"You sound very certain."

"I am," she said, and went to where a leather pouchbag was sitting on a chair near the windows. Behind her, the sky stretched wide and black across Calusa Bay. She reached into the bag and took from it a white, legal-sized envelope. "I got this from Michael last week," she said. "I think you ought to read it."

The envelope was addressed in typescript to Miss Karin Purchase at her address on Central Park West. Michael's return address was in the upper left-hand corner. I opened the already torn flap, and removed from the envelope four typewritten pages folded around another squarish, oatmeal-colored envelope that had in turn been folded to fit inside the letter. This second envelope was addressed by hand to Michael at Pirate's Cove. The monogram on the torn flap was BJP.

"My mother," Karin said.

"Which should I read first?"

"Michael's letter. It makes references to hers."

I took Karin's bag from the seat of the chair, put it on the floor, sat, and was starting to read the letter when a knock sounded on the door. Karin went to open it. A bellman came in with a tray on which were two snifters, two glasses of water, and a check.

"Good evening," he said.

"Good evening," Karin said. "Just put it there, please, on the dresser."

He put down the tray. Karin scarcely glanced at the check. She scrawled a tip and her signature onto it, and then said, "Thank you."

"Thank *you,* miss," the bellman said. His eyes avoided mine. This was five minutes past midnight, the lady was casually dressed, she had ordered drinks in her room for two. The bellman knew an assignation when he saw one. Not for nothing was he nineteen years old and growing a mustache. He backed his way discreetly out of the room. Karin closed and locked the door behind him. She brought me my cognac, went back to the dresser for her own snifter, and then sat on the arm of the chair.

"May I read over your shoulder?" she asked.

"Yes, certainly."

The letter was dated Wednesday, February 25.

Dear Sis,

I don't know what to do about this latest letter from Mom. As you can see, what she's trying to do again is get me involved in her problems with Pop. This time it's because he's cut off alimony payments. I don't know what the hell she expects me to do, I really don't. I'm living on Pop's boat, does she want me to go to him and tell him he should start paying her the alimony again? He'd kick me off the boat for sure, and I can't afford that right now, especially when I'm saving money for tuition in the fall. Anyway, Kar, I'm not even sure I agree with Mom this time.

He's been married to Maureen for eight years now, he's got a new family and a new life. His only ties to Mom were those checks he sent each month. I had a long talk with Maureen last night. Mostly about going back to school, but we also talked about the alimony. Kar, it really was a terrific burden on Pop. He was working harder than he ever had before, going to the office every Wednesday, for example, which used to be his day off, turning off the phone and catching up on paperwork he doesn't have a chance to get to during the week because he's increased his case load so much.

Maureen told me they took only one vacation last year, to Montreal for a week. You know Pop, he really likes his vacations. But here he is taking just a week, and you know as well as I that Mom spent six weeks in Italy last summer and two weeks skiing in Austria this Christmas. She got a two-hundred-thousand-dollar cash settlement, and the interest on that, if she invested it in anything but buggy whips, would have to bring a conservative eight percent a year. I wish I could get that kind of money for doing nothing but being alive. Somebody's suffering for sure, Kar, but I don't think it's Mom, and I really think Pop had every right to tell her to go to hell. He's got a life of his own to lead and he wants to lead it without any ties to a woman he never even thinks about anymore.

My point, Sis, is that Mom has been doing the same number for ten years now, and she does it all over again in the letter I'm enclosing. I love her to death, and I'd do anything in the world for her, I mean it. But that's partly because she's made me feel so goddamn sorry for her, playing the widowed old lady when she's only forty-two! I don't know what to do, Karin, I really don't. I think I'm going to call her and tell her to give it up, let Pop go, for Christ's sake! But then I'm afraid she'll start bawling, and I never know what to do when she cries. Sis, please read her letter and let me know what you think I should tell her. I may call her before I hear from you, because you know Mom, she gets frantic if she thinks she's being neglected.

Love ya,
Michael

P.S. Maureen's birthday is the twelfth of March, it would be nice if you dropped her a card.

"Well?" Karin said, and moved swiftly off the arm of the chair.

"I'd like to read your mother's letter, too."

"The important letter is Michael's," she said. She was already at the dresser, taking a fresh cigarette from the package there, lighting it. "Does that sound like someone about to commit murder?"

"No, it doesn't."

Across the room, Karin sat now in the chair near the television set. She seemed content she'd made her point. There was on her face a look bordering smugness; the trip to Calusa had not been wasted, she had placed into the hands of her brother's attorney a document that would surely save his life. I took her mother's letter from the oatmeal-colored envelope, and unfolded it. The BJP monogram was on the center of the page. There was a brown border running around the entire sheet of stationery. Betty Purchase had written her letter in darker brown ink. It was dated Saturday, February 21. Michael had undoubtedly received it early last week, and had immediately written to his sister on Wednesday, the twenty-fifth, four days before the murders.

Dear Michael,

As I told you on the phone, this will now be the second month your father has defaulted on his alimony payments. He is supposed to send me my check *by the fifteenth, it is supposed to be here in my hands by the fifteenth of each month. A check for $2,500 each month. Today is the 21st, I waited till this morning to write you because I wanted to make sure the check wasn't in the mail. Well, it wasn't.*

In a conversation I had with your father last month when the January check didn't arrive, he told me he was never going to pay me again. I am certain of that now, Michael. Which means I will have to take him to court and spend a lot of money trying to get what is rightfully mine, while he and Goldilocks live in luxury. I want you to go to him, Michael, he won't listen to me, and tell him it's his legal obligation to make those payments each month. He wanted his freedom, and I gave it to him, but he also signed an agreement that I expect him to honor. I was once his wife, Michael. He seems to have forgotten that.

He seems to have forgotten, too, that I was the one who had the paying job that put him through medical school. So I believe I'm entitled to a small share of his income now. I'm not a demanding woman, Michael, I didn't make punitive demands. I wish you would go see him, and take him aside where Goldilocks can't hear you, and ask him to please send me my money. I would appreciate it, son. Please call me when you receive this, as I want to know whether you plan to help me or not.

All my love,
Mother

I folded the letter and put it back into the envelope. I put the envelope and Michael's letter back into the larger envelope. I picked up the snifter again, and sipped at the cognac. "*Did* Michael call her?" I asked.

"Yes."

"How do you know?"

"When I got this letter—"

"When was that?"

"Saturday morning. I called my mother immediately. She told me she'd already spoken to Michael, and he'd said he wouldn't do what she'd asked."

"What did she plan to do next?"

"Take my father to court, what *else* could she do? I think you're missing the point, Mr. Hope. The point is that Michael had already turned down my mother's plea. Michael had already sided with Maureen and my father. Do you understand what I'm saying? He could *not* have committed those murders."

"Perhaps not," I said. "Have you spoken to your mother since that call Saturday morning?"

"No. I tried to reach her last night, from New York, but she was out. I was planning to call tonight, but the plane got in late, and I didn't want to wake her. She's normally in bed by nine, nine-thirty."

"Then she doesn't know you're here in Calusa."

"No, she doesn't. I'll call her first thing tomorrow morning."

"Have you spoken to your father yet?"

"No."

"Why not?"

"I don't want to," Karin said, and shrugged almost childishly.

"Why not?"

"Because I think . . . well, never mind."

"What is it you think, Miss Purchase?"

"Nothing."

"I'd like to know."

"Let me just give you the facts. You're an attorney, you put the facts together, okay? Fact number one," she said ticking it off on the pinky of her left hand, "Dad has another woman. He's only been married to Maureen for eight years, but he's already playing around with another woman."

"How do you know that?"

"He told me all about her. When I saw him at Christmas."

"He told *you?*"

"Don't be so shocked. He had to tell someone, and I was available. I'm a very good listener. Especially with older men," she said, and smiled. "Fact number two, he's very serious about this woman, and was planning to leave Maureen for her. Fact number three," she said, ticking it off on her middle finger, "my dear father doesn't like paying alimony, as witness the recent cutting off of funds to my mother. If and when he left Maureen—excuse me, this is fact number four—he'd have been in court with two ex-wives at the same time, and might have ended up paying alimony to *both* of them, not to mention support money for the little girls. Those are the facts, Mr. Hope," she said, holding up the four spread fingers. "Think about them."

I thought about them. My mind soared with possibilities. Jamie wanted to be rid of Maureen, but he'd been burned before, his former wife had refused to negotiate with him for eighteen months, and had finally saddled him with an unbearable settlement agreement. He'd quit paying alimony to her in January, and he wasn't ready to start negotiating with yet *another* woman he no longer loved. So he and Catherine in their cottage by the sea had mentioned *murder,* had dared to whisper *murder* against the whisper of the surf, *murder, murder,* and the idea had grown, had become justified, had finally become reasonable and inevitable. Last night, he left the poker game early. He went home to the house on Jacaranda to kill Maureen—

And his daughters?

No.

Impossible.

Simply and utterly impossible.

"No," I said. "I don't think so, Miss Purchase."

"No? Then who's Michael protecting?"

I did not venture the suggestion that Michael might very well be protecting his mother, Betty Purchase. I said only, "Perhaps no one. Perhaps he *did* kill them."

"You read his letter," Karin said.

"Yes."

"And you can still think that?"

"I don't know what to think," I said, and looked at my watch.

"Another drink?" Karin said at once. "Shall I phone down?"

"No, thank you, I've got to be going," I said, and put the letters in my pocket.

"Will you show those to the police?"

"Yes."

"I don't seem to have convinced you," she said, and smiled tightly.

"Of what? Your brother's innocence, or your father's guilt?"

"You don't know my father as well as I do. You don't know how cruel he can be."

"I don't think he's a murderer," I said, and rose, and walked to the door.

"Once you've divorced a wife of fifteen years, anything else is easy," Karin said.

"Not murder, Miss Purchase. Good night, I appreciate your—"

"Even murder."

"Not killing your own daughters," I said, and opened the door.

"Divorce *is* a kind of killing," she said.

13

It was a quarter to one when I got back to the house. The lights in the study were on. Susan was sitting naked behind the desk. Her left hand was on the telephone. She said nothing as I stopped in the doorway and looked into the room.

"What is it?" I said.

A faint smile touched her mouth.

"Susan?"

"I just had a phone call," she said.

"Who from?"

"A man named Gerald Hemmings."

My throat went suddenly dry. In the beginning, Aggie and I had rehearsed this scene a thousand times. We knew exactly what to say in the event of a trap. Since we were both sworn to secrecy, confrontation could only be a trap. Whatever Susan or Gerald might say in accusation, we were to respond with a lie. But that was in the beginning. This was here and now. Last month, we'd agreed to tell them both; there was no need for denial now.

"Gerald Hemmings?" I said. "I don't think I know him. What'd he want at this hour?"

"He wanted to talk to you. He talked to me instead."

I said nothing. I waited. I knew this was not a trap.

But it had to be a trap. But I knew it wasn't. Had someone seen us? That woman on the beach this afternoon, the one collecting shells? Had she seen me going into the house? Had she recognized me? Had she called Gerald Hemmings to tell him? I waited. The silence lengthened. Susan kept staring at me.

"Well, I . . . who *is* this man?" I said. "I've never—"

"We met his wife at the theater."

"His wife?"

"Agatha Hemmings."

It was the first time her name had ever been mentioned in this house. It did not come as a surprise, but it exploded into the room nonetheless, shrapnel flying into every corner, *Agatha Hemmings,* ricocheting from the walls, *Agatha Hemmings,* maiming, blinding.

"I don't remember her," I said.

"Mr. Hemmings seems to think you're having an affair with her."

"What are you talking about?"

"Agatha Hemmings. Her husband seems to think—"

"Yes, I heard you. But—"

"But of course it isn't true."

"Now come on, Susan. I don't know who called you tonight, but—"

"Mr. Hemmings called me."

"Or at least someone who *said* he was Mr. Hemmings."

"Yes, someone who gave a very good imitation of Mr. Hemmings telling me you've been fucking his wife, yes."

"Susan, I don't know what this is all about, I swear to God."

"Don't swear to God, Matthew. He'll send down a lightning bolt."

"I'm glad you find this comical. A man calls in the middle of the night—"

"Oh yes, very comical."

"Well, I'm certainly glad—"

"Hilarious, in fact. I even asked Mr. Hemmings if this was some kind of joke. That's because I found it so side-splitting, Matthew. Mr. Hemmings didn't think it was funny, though. He kept crying all the while he talked to me. There were times I couldn't understand what he was saying, Matthew. But I got the gist of it. I managed to get the gist of it. Would you like to hear the gist of it, Matthew?"

"No, I'd like to go to sleep. We'll talk about this in—"

"We'll talk about it *now*, you son of a bitch!"

"There's nothing to talk about, Susan."

"That's right, Matthew. Afer tonight, there's nothing to talk about ever again. But there's *this* to talk about now."

"I don't want to hear it."

"You'll hear it, or I'll wake Joanna and tell *her* about it. Would you like your daughter to hear it, Matthew?"

"What do you want, Susan? If you're so sure that whoever called was telling the truth—"

"He was telling the truth."

"Fine, then. *You* believe it, okay? *I'm* going to—"

"She tried to kill herself, Matthew."

"What?"

"She swallowed half a bottle of sleeping pills."

"Who . . . did he tell you that?"

"Yes."

"I don't believe you."

"Call her. Ask her."

"Why should . . . I don't know her, I don't even remember meeting—"

"Matthew, she tried to *kill* herself! Now, for Christ's sake, are you going to keep—"

"All right," I said.

"Ah."

"When did he call?"

"About ten minutes ago."

"Is she . . . is she all right?"

"I thought you'd never ask."

"Look, Susan—"

"Don't look *me*, you bastard!"

"What happened? Are you going to tell me what happened or—"

"He'd been watching television. He went upstairs at eleven and found her unconscious."

"Did he call a doctor?"

"No."

"Why not?"

"He could see what she'd done, there were pills all over the floor. He forced her to vomit, he put her under a cold shower, and then he marched her up and down the bedroom. That's when she told him everything, Matthew. While they were walking back and forth, back and forth." She made her voice mincingly precious on the repeated words "back and forth," walking the index and middle fingers of her right hand across the top of the desk, across a sheaf of papers, over a pair of scissors, and then back toward the telephone again, "Back and forth, back and forth." I watched her fingers and visualized Aggie clinging limply to her husband as he tried to walk off the effect of the pills. Her hair would have been wet from the shower, her face ghostly white, the pale gray eyes drained of whatever pigment they ordinarily possessed. And she would be talking. She would be telling.

"Okay," I said.

"Okay?" Susan stopped the walking fingers, clenched her right hand into a fist, and put it abruptly in her lap. "What does that mean, Matthew, okay?"

"It means okay, now I know what happened."

"But you don't know *why* it happened. You don't know *why* she took all those pills, do you?"

"Why did she take them, Susan?"

"Because she was convinced you wouldn't ask me for a divorce," Susan said, and burst out laughing. Her laughter was frightening, I had the sudden premonition that another nightmare was about to start, that perhaps it had started the moment I entered the house and saw the study lights burning. Or before that, perhaps—the shrill ringing of the telephone, Susan coming down the hall naked to answer it in the study, *I'm sorry, Mr. Hemmings, he's not here just now,* and the nightmare was suddenly full-blown upon her, upon us.

I came around the desk swiftly, wanting to stop her manic laughter before it woke up Joanna just down the hall. I put my hand on her shoulder, and she recoiled from it as though a lizard had crawled up her arm. The laughter stopped abruptly, but suddenly there was more to be afraid of than hysterical laughter. Without warning her hand reached out. She picked up the scissors. Her arm swung around in an arc, she came up out of the black leather swivel chair in the same instant, so that the motions were linked and seemed like one, sideward and upward.

The thumb- and finger-loops of the scissors were clutched in her fist like the haft of a dagger. She came at me without hesitation, propelled by fury, mindlessly. The twin pointed tips of the blades were an inch from my belly when I caught her wrist and deflected the forward thrust. She pulled her arm free, lunged again, and this time succeeded in ripping the sleeve of my jacket. Her breathing was harsh and ragged, I was not sure she even remembered the cause of her anger anymore. But still she lashed out with the scissors, coming at me again and again, forcing me back against the bookcase wall, causing me to sidle along it like a crab. I could not catch her wrist, her hand moved too swiftly, the tips of the scissors flicking the air and retreating, flicking again, catching the lapel of my jacket, clinging there an instant till she ripped them free with a twist and came at me again. I brought up my left hand, and a gash suddenly opened from my knuckles to my wrist. I felt suddenly faint and fell against the desk for support, knocking the telephone to the floor. She was on me again, I recalled abruptly Jamie's description of the bedroom on Jacaranda, the blood-smeared walls, Maureen fluttering to—

There was a scream.

For a moment, I thought I was the one screaming. My bleeding hand was stretched toward Susan, my mouth was indeed open—it was possible that I was the one screaming. But the scream was coming from behind me. I spun to my left, partially to avoid the thrusting scissors, partially to locate the source of the scream. My daughter Joanna was standing in the open doorway. She was wearing a long granny nightgown, her eyes were wide, her mouth was open, the scream that came from her throat could have raised the dead. It was a scream of horror and disbelief, it hung on the air interminably, it filled the small room and suffocated murderous intent. The scissors stopped. Susan looked down at her own right hand in disbelief. It was shaking violently, the scissors jerking erratically in her fist. She dropped them to the floor.

"Get out," she said. "Get out, you bastard."

Inexplicably, Joanna rushed to her and threw herself into her arms.

Sunlight streamed through the partially opened blinds. I cracked open my eyes and blinked at the morning. I was on the couch in my office. The wall clock read 8:15 A.M. The nightmare was over.

I looked at my bandaged left hand. The blood had soaked through and crusted the cotton gauze. I sat up. For a moment, I did not want to get off that couch; there seemed no place to go. I thought of my daughter in Susan's arms. The image persisted. I shook my head as though to clear it, got to my feet, and looked at the clock again. My clothes were rumpled, I had slept in them. I was barefooted. My shoes were resting side by side before the desk, the socks bunched inside them. I hated the thought of showering and then putting on again the same clothes I'd worn through last night's horror. But I'd left the house with only what was on my back. Turned, walked out of the study, through the hallway to the front door, the door whispering shut behind me, the small click of the snap lock in the strike plate. *Click.* My daughter in Susan's arms. Her *mother's* arms, not mine.

I crossed the office now, and opened the door, and went down the hall to the shower. I put the suit on a hanger, in hope that the steam would take out some of the wrinkles. There was nothing to be done about the shirt, I would have to wear it again as it was. The socks really bothered me, though, the prospect of putting on socks I'd worn the day before. But there was no way to wash them and have them dry in time to start the day. I wondered how to start the day. The water was hot, the steam rose around me, enveloping me. I would have to call Aggie. Gerald and the children would be gone by—but what difference did it make? Gerald knew. Was it now possible to call the house and say, "Hi, this is Matthew Hope, may I please speak to Aggie?"

I tried to tell myself that none of last night had happened.

The steam rose obligingly, misting the shower stall and the world beyond. I thought of my daughter. Thought of her rushing into Susan's arms. Did all of them rush into their mothers' arms after a divorce or a separation? Karin Purchase not wanting to call her father. Called her mother from New York the minute she got Michael's letter, and tried her again the following night, but wouldn't call her father even though she was here in Calusa now, local call, pick up the phone, Hello, Dad, this is Karin. No. Would Joanna ever call me?

Under the shower, I began weeping.

It was ten minutes to nine by the time I finished shaving. I did not feel much better. The wrinkles had come out of my suit, but the shirt felt stale with yesterday. I had not yet put on the socks. I did not want to put on the socks. I dialed Aggie's number. The phone began ringing on the other end. Once, twice, again, again. My hand was sweating on the receiver. I did not want to talk to Gerald Hemmings. The phone kept ringing. I was about to hang up when her voice said, "Hello?" Barely a whisper. I thought at once that he was still in the house. I thought she was answering in some secret corner, whispering.

"Aggie?"

"Yes."

"Are you alone?"

"Yes."

"What happened?"

"It just seemed . . . I'm sorry, Matthew, forgive me," she said, and began crying.

I waited.

"Aggie," I said.

"Yes, darling."

She was sobbing into the phone. I saw Susan's fingers marching across the desk again, saw Aggie in the arms of her husband as he walked her back into life.

"Tell me what happened."

"I thought . . ." She gasped for breath, I was suddenly impatient with her. And angry. At her? At myself?

"Thought what?"

"That you'd . . . never tell her. I—"

"Aggie, I *promised* you!"

"I know, but . . ." She caught her breath on a sob. There was a silence, long and deep. I waited. She blew her nose. The sound trumpeted into the telephone, I suddenly saw her red-eyed and weepy. "Alone last night," she said, and began crying again. I looked at the clock. It was five minutes to nine, I wanted her to get off the phone. I wanted her to tell me what the hell had happened, and get off the phone. I did not want her to be on the phone when my partner Frank walked into the office. What would I tell him? What would my cynical New Yorker friend say when I told him Susan had come at me with a pair of scissors last night? What would he say when I told him I'd been having an affair with Agatha Hemmings since May of last year?

"Aggie, why'd you tell him?"

"Because I knew it was over."

"*What* was over? How could you think that? I promised you yesterday afternoon—"

"But you wouldn't tell her."

"I *said* I'd tell her!"

"But you *didn't!*"

"Shit, Aggie—"

"Don't you care that I tried to kill myself?"

"You know I do, for God's sake—"

"I was listening to the radio."

"What?"

"When I did it. They were playing a Stravinsky piano quartet, I don't know which one. They have chamber music on Monday nights. He was downstairs watching television, I was reading and listening to the music when suddenly I knew you'd never do it, I just knew you'd never tell her. I went . . . I got out of bed and went into the bathroom—I was wearing the peignoir you gave me last Christmas, the one I said my mother sent from Cambridge, the blue one with the lace trim. There were pills I had from when Julia was sick with the whooping cough and I couldn't sleep nights. I took them back to bed with me, I swallowed them without water, just kept throwing them way back into my mouth until . . ." She was sobbing again. "You see, Matthew, it all seemed so useless. My life without you. Useless."

"What are we going to do now?"

"I don't know, Matthew. What are we going to do?"

"I don't know."

"When *will* you know?"

"I need time to—"

"I don't *have* time," she said, and hung up.

There was a hollow click, and then silence. I pressed one of the cradle-rest buttons, got a dial tone, and called her back. The phone kept ringing. I let it ring. I was suddenly afraid that the rest of those pills—

"Hello?"

"Aggie, don't hang up again."

"What do you want, Matthew?"

"When can I see you?"

"Why do you want to see me?"

"We have a lot to talk about."

"Do we?"

"You know we do."

"I'm not sure."

"Aggie, for the love of God—"

"Make up your mind," she said. "Call me when you make up your mind."

"Don't hang up, Aggie."

"Yes, I'm going to," she said.

"Aggie—"

The line went dead.

I put the receiver back on the cradle, and sat there with my hand on the phone, staring at the phone, wondering how many minutes, how many hours Aggie and I had stolen on the telephone together over the past year. Secret calls from the office, calls from phone booths all over town, how would it be without those calls—*Call me when you make up your mind.* I lifted the receiver again, I put it down again, I rose from the desk and began pacing my office.

There were things to do this morning, things I had to do. Michael, I had to see Michael. I wanted to talk to him about that letter he'd written to his sister, yes, and the phone call he'd made to his mother. Told her he wouldn't intercede on her behalf. In effect, go to hell, Mom, I won't go talk to Pop about the goddamn alimony—called his father Pop. Joanna called me Dad or Daddy, what did *Karin* call *her* father? Dad, right. Fact number one, Dad has another woman. Didn't phone him, though, oh no, saved all the loving phone calls for Mom, never mind Dad who had another woman. Called Mom Saturday morning, planned to call her again first thing this morning because the plane—*I tried to reach her last night, from New York, but she was out.*

Karin had been talking about Sunday night. Sunday night—when Maureen and the two little girls were stabbed to death. Sunday night—when Betty Purchase was supposed to have been home watching television.

I tried to reach her last night, from New York, but she was out.

I was suddenly wide awake.

She was wearing a robe over her nightgown when finally she answered the door. I'd been ringing the bell for five minutes, pounding on the door for another five after that, and now she opened the door and peered out at me, blinking her eyes against the sunshine. She wore no makeup; her face was still puffed with sleep. "I'm sorry to bother you," I said, "but there are some questions I have to ask."

"What time is it?" she said.

"Nine-thirty."

"Come back later," she said, and started to close the door.

"No, Betty. *Now.*"

She sighed in annoyance, and then turned her back and walked into the house. I followed her into a living room furnished in stark modern, all cool blues and whites, an abstract painting dominating the fireplace wall, angles and slashes in reds and oranges. There were two closed doors at the far end of the room. Beyond the sliding glass doors opposite the fireplace was the deck, and beyond that the ocean.

"Betty," I said, "where were you Sunday night?"

"Here."

"No."

"I was here," she said flatly. "I was watching television all night long."

"From when to when?"

"All night."

"No," I said, and shook my head.

"What is this, Matt? I've already told the police where—"

"You weren't here, Betty. Your daughter tried to call you from New York. She got no answer. Where were you?"

"If the police have any further—"

"Never mind the police! Your son is sitting downtown in a goddamn jail cell, and he's confessed to murder, and I want to know where you were Sunday night. Was it you who called Michael at the marina?"

"No. Called him? What are you talking about?"

"Did you ask him to meet you at Jamie's house? Were you at Jamie's house Sunday night? Where were you, Betty?"

"Here," she said. Her lips were beginning to tremble. Her hands were clasped tightly in her lap. "Here," she said again.

"Okay," I said, "have it your way. I'm going to tell Ehrenberg you lied to him. I'm going to tell him your daughter tried to phone you Sunday night and got no answer. I'm going to ask him to find out just *where* the hell you were, because it might have been on Sabal Shores, killing—"

"She was with *me*."

I turned abruptly. One of the doors at the far end of the room was open now. The woman who stood in the doorframe was perhaps forty years old, a tall, wide-shouldered redhead, her face sprinkled with freckles, her arms folded over ample breasts, thick legs showing beneath the hem of a baby doll nightgown.

Betty rose from where she was sitting, her hand outstretched as though to physically push the woman back beyond that open door fifteen feet across the room. "Jackie, please," she said.

"Please, my ass," Jackie said. "He's trying to tie you to those fucking murders."

"Please," Betty said.

"She was with *me,* mister. She picked me up in a bar on Lucy's Key, and we went to my place afterwards. *That's* where she was Sunday night."

I remembered what Jamie had told me about the first frigid years of his marriage. I remembered what Betty had told me only yesterday about the difficulties of finding available men in this town full of divorcées and widows. I remembered what she'd said about protecting her reputation here, about not wanting anyone snooping into her private life. And it suddenly seemed entirely plausible that she would have lied to the police about where she *actually* was Sunday night, rather than admit she'd been with a woman she'd picked up in a bar.

"Okay," I said. "I'm sorry."

"So fuck off," Jackie said.

Michael was sitting in his cell at the end of the corridor. It was ten-thirty A.M., he had eaten breakfast at seven, and was waiting to be transferred to the jail across the street. I'd called Ehrenberg ten minutes earlier, and he'd told me to get over there right away if I wanted to talk to him before he was moved. Michael did not seem overjoyed to see me.

"Your sister's in town," I said. "I talked to her last night."

"Good," he said, and nodded.

"She gave me the letter you wrote her. I'll be showing it to the police."

"Why'd she do that?"

"She was trying to help you."

"She can help me by keeping her nose out of this."

"I have some questions for you, Michael."

"I don't want to answer any questions. Why'd they

let you in here, anyway? Don't I have any say about who's—"

"In your letter, you—"

"Jesus!"

"In your letter, you didn't sound like someone even remotely considering murder. In fact, you even reminded your—"

"I don't care *what* I sounded like in a letter."

"You reminded your sister that Maureen's birthday was coming. You asked her to send a card. Do you remember that?"

"Yes, I remember it."

"If you were planning to kill Maureen—"

"I wasn't *planning* anything!"

"Then it was a spur of the moment thing, is that it?"

"Yes, that's what it was. I told you what it was. Why don't you go listen to the tape? It's all on the tape, what the hell more do you want?"

"I want to know why."

"I don't know why."

"Tell me what Maureen said to you on the phone."

"I told you what she said. She said she was afraid, and she wanted me to come to the house."

"What was she afraid of?"

"She didn't say."

"She just said she was afraid."

"Yes."

"But not of what."

"She said she didn't know what to do."

"About *what?* Michael, you're only repeating—"

"It's what she *said*, damn it!"

"She said she didn't know what to do."

"That's right."

"And you didn't ask her about what. A person says, 'I don't know what to do'—"

"That's right, I didn't ask her."

"You weren't even curious."

"No."

"But you went to the house."

"You *know* I went to the house."

"Why?"

"Because she was scared."

"And she didn't know what to do."

"That's right."

"But she never told you what was frightening her, or what it was she—"

"Listen, you're not going to trick me," he said suddenly.

"Trick you?"

"You heard me."

"Into what?"

"Nothing."

"No one's trying to trick you, Michael."

"Okay."

"Believe me."

"Okay, then why don't you just go home, okay? I don't want to talk about Maureen anymore, okay?"

"Why'd you ask your sister to send her a card?"

"I just told you I don't want to—"

"Did *you* plan to send a card, too?"

"No. I was going to buy her something."

"What?"

"What difference does it make?" he said. "She's dead."

"Michael . . . when you got to the house that night, what did you talk about?"

"I don't remember."

"You went into the kitchen, you sat at the kitchen table. Isn't that what you said?"

"That's right."

"What did you talk about?"

"I don't know."

"Did you talk about going back to school?"

"Yes. That's right, we talked about going back to school. And about the alimony, about Pop stopping the alimony."

He had a way of seizing upon suggestions and turning them into his own responses. A moment before, he could not remember what he and Maureen had talked about. But now that I'd provided a possible subject matter, he accepted it at once and was ready to expand upon it. Had I asked that same question of my own client in a court of law, the opposing attorney would have leaped to his feet at once, to object that I was leading the witness. I decided to be more careful with him.

"Until what time did you talk, Michael?"

"Until . . . late. I don't have a watch."

"Then how do you know it was late?"

"Well . . . she *said* it was late."

"Who said it was late?"

"Maureen."

"Then what?"

"I don't know what."

"When did you reach for the knife?"

"I don't remember. I told you I don't remember."

"Michael, at some point in that conversation with Maureen, you got up from the table and reached for a knife. That's what you told Ehrenberg in your statement. I want to know why. I want to know what was said that caused you to—"

"Nothing. Go to hell. Nothing was said."

"You just reached up for the knife?"

"Yes."

"Just like that."

"I don't remember."

"You just told me Maureen said it was late—"

"She said she was going to bed, it was late."

"Is that what she said exactly? Can you remember?"

"She said she . . . she had a busy day tomorrow and . . . it was getting late and she was going to bed."

"That sounds like—"

"That's what she said."

He was at the house only last Tuesday, he and Maureen sat at the kitchen table half the night, just talking. A real heart-to-heart talk. About my having stopped the alimony payments, about his going back to school—they'd have gone on forever if I hadn't told them I was going to bed, I had a busy day tomorrow.

"It sounds like what your *father* said."

"My father wasn't there."

"Not *Sunday* night, Michael, *Tuesday* night. When you and Maureen talked for hours at the kitchen table."

"We . . . talked Sunday night, too."

"Did you?"

"Yes. I told you we—"

"During all the time you talked, did you once ask her what she was afraid of?"

"No."

"But you said that was the reason you went to the house."

"That's right."

"You hitched a ride from the end of Stone Crab Key—"

"Yes."

"Because Maureen was afraid of something—"

"That's—"

"But then you killed her."

He did not answer.

"Michael?"

He still did not answer.

"Michael, who called you on Sunday night?"

"Maureen. I told you it was Maureen."

"Michael, I don't think Maureen called you. I think Maureen was dead when you got there."

He shook his head.

"Who killed her, Michael? Do you know who killed her?"

At the far end of the corridor, there was the sound of the door clanging open, and then hurried footsteps. I turned at once. Ehrenberg was approaching the cell.

"You'd better come upstairs," he said. "We've got another confession in this damn case."

14

"SHE CAME in five minutes ago," Ehrenberg said, "told the girl downstairs she wanted to talk to whoever was in charge of the Purchase murder case. Girl sent her right up. I introduced myself, and the first thing she said was, 'I killed them.' She started filling me in, and I stopped her cold, put in a call to the captain. He told me to call the State's Attorney's office, we want *them* here doing the interview. We can't afford any foul-ups on this. If we have two confessions kicking around, we may end up with nobody getting blamed for the crime. I'll tell you, I never did buy that boy's story all the way, too many loose ends that kept unraveling."

We had come down the corridor and into the reception area. The orange letter-elevator still dominated the room, the girl was still behind her desk typing. Ehrenberg asked her if the captain had arrived yet, and she told him he hadn't.

"She's in there waiting to talk to you," he said, and indicated the door to the captain's office.

She was sitting in the same chair Michael had sat in yesterday morning. She was wearing a dark blue linen suit and blue patent leather pumps. Her blonde hair was pulled into a severe bun at the back of her head. She looked up as I came into the room.

"I wanted you here when I exonerated my brother," she said. "Detective Ehrenberg told me you were right downstairs."

"Yes. Talking to Michael, in fact."

"How is he?" Her eyes searched my face—her father's eyes, Jamie's eyes.

"He seems all right," I said. "Miss Purchase, you told Detective Ehrenberg you killed Maureen and her daughters. Is that—"

"Yes."

"Is that true?"

"Yes, it's true."

"Because if it isn't, you won't be doing Michael a damn bit of good by confessing to a crime you didn't commit."

"Mr. Hope, I killed them," she said. The pale blue eyes fastened on mine. "Believe me, I killed them."

By eleven-fifteen, they had all gathered and were ready to discuss it. They were experts all of them, and they knew that the progress of an interview, as they insisted on calling it, could be seriously impeded by the presence of too many "authority figures," as the man from the State's Attorney's office labeled us. I was one of the authority figures; Karin Purchase had stated plainly that she would not make a statement unless her brother's attorney were there to hear every word. The captain in charge of the Detective Bureau wisely offered to stay out of the questioning session, offering the opinion that Miss Purchase now knew Ehrenberg was the man in charge of the investigation, and might feel more comfortable in his presence.

The man from the State's Attorney's office was a stout and perspiring gentleman named Roger Bensell. He was wearing a winter-weight brown pin-striped suit, with a yellow shirt and a maroon tie. His shoes were brown, with perforated pointed tips that made him look like a fat ballroom dancer. He kept mopping his brow and telling the captain that this was an important case. I had no doubt that both the captain and Ehrenberg were well aware of this; the very fact that the State's Attorney was here seemed to prove that contention. It was decided that Ehrenberg and I would both be in attendance while Bensell conducted the interview. The captain informed Karin of this, and she was entirely agreeable.

He further suggested that since the rooms customarily used for interviewing were somewhat smaller than might allow for the comfort of four people, Karin might prefer being interviewed there in his own office. Karin accepted his offer. The captain introduced her to Mr. Bensell of the State's Attorney's office, and left the room. Mr. Bensell asked if she was ready to begin. She said she was. He pushed the RECORD button on the tape recorder and, just as Ehrenberg had done yesterday, told the microphone what day it was, and what time—eleven-twenty A.M.—and where we were, and who was present. He then laboriously read her rights to her, and Karin acknowledged that she understood each and every one of them, and said that the only attorney she wished present during the interview was Mr. Matthew Hope. Bensell then began the question-and-answer session.

Q: What is your name, please?
A: Karin Purchase.
Q: Can you tell me where you live, Miss Purchase?
A: In New York City.
Q: Where in New York?
A: Central Park West. 322 Central Park West.
Q: Do you have an address here in Calusa?
A: Right now, I'm staying at the Calusa Bay Hotel.
Q: By right now . . .
A: I moved there last night. When I first arrived in Calusa, I checked into a motel near the airport.
Q: When was that?
A: Sunday night.
Q: By Sunday night, do you mean Sunday, February twenty-ninth?
A: Yes. I know what Mr. Hope is thinking. He's thinking I told him I'd arrived in Calusa only last night. But I was lying to him. I got here on Sunday.

Q: What time Sunday?

A: I took a flight from Newark at five-forty-five. I arrived in Calusa at a little past ten. I called my mother from the airport, I was planning to stay with her, but she was out. So I rented a car and looked for a motel.

Q: Why did you come to Calusa, Miss Purchase?

A: To talk to my mother.

Q: About what?

A: About the alimony payments. My father stopped the alimony payments. When I spoke to her on the phone Saturday, she was very upset. I decided to come down and talk to her personally. To try to comfort her. To figure out what we should do next. But she wasn't home.

Q: So you checked into a motel instead.

A: Yes.

Q: Can you tell me the name of the motel?

A: Twin Ridges? Something like that. I don't remember.

Q: What time did you check in?

A: It must've been close to ten-thirty.

Q: What did you do then?

A: I tried to reach my mother again. She was still out.

Q: Yes, go on.

A: I watched television for a little while. Then I tried her again, and there was still no answer. I was very eager to talk to her. It was my idea to confront my father. To go there together with my mother and demand . . . you see, my brother had already told her he wouldn't help her. But she wasn't home.

Q: This was what time, Miss Purchase?

A: I'm not sure. A quarter to eleven, I would guess.

Q: What did you do then? When you couldn't get your mother on the telephone.

A: I decided I'd go see my father alone. Without her. I knew just what I wanted to tell him, I didn't need her with me.

Q: What did you want to tell him?

A: What do you think? That he had to pay the alimony. It was hers. They'd agreed to it. She *deserved* it.

Q: Did you, in fact, go to see your father?

A: Yes.

Q: You went to your father's house on Jacaranda Drive?
A: Yes.
Q: Did you go there unannounced?
A: Yes. I didn't want to call him because this was something that couldn't be discussed on the telephone.
Q: What time did you get to the house on Jacaranda Drive?
A: Eleven-fifteen or so. I got lost. I don't know Calusa too well.
Q: What did you do when you got there?
A: I parked the car in the driveway, and went to the front door, and rang the bell. There were lights on, I knew they were still up.
Q: They?
A: My father and Goldi—my father and his present wife.
Q: Maureen Purchase?
A: Yes.
Q: *Were* they both in fact there?
A: No. Only Maureen. She was the one who answered the door. She didn't recognize me at first. I had to tell her who I was.
Q: What happened after you identified yourself?
A: She asked me what I wanted. I said I wanted to talk to my father, and she told me he wasn't there.
Q: Then what?
A: I asked her if I could come in. To see for myself that he wasn't there. She said she was just about to go to bed, and I'd have to take her word for it. So I . . . she was starting to close the door. I shoved it open and went inside. She told me to get out, she tried to grab my arm, but I pushed her away and walked into the living room. My father wasn't there, I looked in the bedroom I looked in the kitchen, he wasn't there. I was coming out of the kitchen when I heard her dialing the phone. I guess she was calling the police. Calling the *police* to evict me from my own own . . . my own father's house. . . . There was a knife in the sink, I picked it up, I guess I had the idea of cutting the telephone cord. The phone was on a drop-leaf desk against the wall, she was sitting in a chair at the desk. She'd just finished dialing, she hadn't yet said anything into

the phone. She saw the knife in my hand and hung up right away, and shoved back the chair. The chair fell over, she sort of tripped on it, she was wearing a long pink nightgown, the skirt got tangled in one of the chair legs.

Q: Can you describe the nightgown, please?

A: It was pink nylon, a long flowing gown with a scoop neck and a rosette above the bosom.

Q: What else was she wearing?

A: Just the nightgown.

Q: Any jewelry?

A: A wedding band.

Q: Anything else?

A: Nothing.

Q: What happened after she hung up the phone?

A: She began screaming. I told her to shut up, was she crazy? But she kept screaming. I couldn't stand her screaming like that. I threatened her with the knife—

Q: How?

A: I pushed it at her. I made a threatening gesture. To shut her up.

Q: Then what?

A: She ran past me, for the bedroom. I was afraid there might be an extension phone in there, so I ran after her. I didn't want her calling the police and making false charges. She was trying to lock the door when I got to it, but I was stronger than she was, I simply pushed it open and went into the room. She kept backing away from me, she was really frightened by then, I think she thought I was going to hurt her. There was a walk-in closet opposite the door, at the far end of the bedroom. She ran into it and tried to keep me out, holding that door closed, too, but I pushed it open, and went in after her. There were clothes . . . you should have *seen* the clothes! He'd stopped sending my mother money, but Goldilocks had a closetful of clothes that must've cost a fortune. That's what infuriated me. The clothes.

Q: Go on, Miss Purchase.

A: I stabbed her, that's all.

Q: Go on.

A: She screamed, and I stabbed her again. She got by me somehow, she got into the bedroom again. I went after her, I chased her around the room, cutting her, she was, she kept grabbing for the walls, she got blood all over the walls. Then she ran back into the closet again, and tried to close the door, but I pushed it open, she was bleeding very badly by then. I grabbed her hair and pulled back her head, and cut her throat. She fell to the floor and I just kept stabbing her. And then, yes, I tried to take off her wedding band, but it wouldn't come off. So I began cutting her finger, to get the wedding band off. It wouldn't . . . I couldn't cut through the bone.

Q: Why did you try to take off the wedding band?

A: It wasn't hers. It wasn't rightfully hers. It was my . . . my mother's. It should have been my mother's.

Q: Go on.

A: I heard something behind me, and I turned, and one of the little girls was standing in the door to the room. She'd heard her mother screaming, I guess, she was standing there in a blue nightgown, a baby doll nightgown, with matching panties. I got up, I'd been on my knees trying to get the wedding band off. The little girl turned and ran, and I went after her. I didn't want her . . . I didn't want her telling what she'd seen. She'd seen me. I didn't want her telling. I caught her just inside the door to her room. I stabbed her, and she fell to the floor, and then I stabbed her again to make sure she was dead. I kept stabbing her. The other little girl was still asleep, she'd slept through all the screaming, I couldn't believe it. I went to her bed and stabbed her through the bedclothes. I forget how many times I stabbed her. Three or four times. Until she was dead.

Q: Why did you stab the second child? The first child saw you, but the second child . . .

A: Sleeping there in my bed.

Q: *Your* bed?

A: So I stabbed her. That was it. I stabbed her. Then . . . then I went out to the living room, and picked up the chair Goldilocks had knocked over, and sat in it and decided I'd better call my brother for help. But there was blood all over my hands, I didn't want to get blood on the telephone, it was a white telephone. So I went back into the bedroom, *her* bedroom, and washed my hands in the bathroom there, and dried them on a towel, a green towel. Then I went out to the living room again. There was a phone book on the desk. Two numbers were listed for Pirate's Cove, one for the restaurant and the other for the marina. I called the marina number and whoever answered the phone said he would get Michael for me. When Michael came to the phone, I told him I was alone there with Goldilocks and the little girls. I told him they were dead, I told him I'd killed them. He told me to wait there, he'd be right there.

Q: Did you wait for him?

A: I waited for ten minutes.

Q: Then what?

A: I got frightened. First I thought I heard one of the little girls moaning in the bedroom, and I went in there to make sure they were dead, and they were. But I kept hearing the moaning. So I went in to look at *her* again—it seemed like the sounds were coming from *her* bedroom now—but she was lying there on the floor of the closet, dead, staring up at me, her mouth open . . . it frightened me. Later, when I had a chance to think about it, I decided that . . . that the sounds were probably some animal outside. But it sounded like moaning. I thought one of them was moaning. So I ran out of the house.

Q: Weren't you worried that your brother might later enter the house and be found there by the police?

A: I didn't think he'd go in. Why would he go in?

Q: Because you told him you'd be waiting there.

A: Yes, but he wouldn't go in. If he saw my car was gone . . . if he saw there weren't any cars in the driveway . . . well, he'd have to know I didn't *walk* there. So he'd know I was gone. He wouldn't go in. Anyway, it never entered my mind. I figured he'd just come there and see I was gone . . . it never entered my mind. I was frightened. I didn't want to stay in that house another moment.

Q: What time was it when you left?

A: Twenty to twelve. I looked at the kitchen clock.

Q: Did you leave by the front door?

A: No. I was afraid someone might see me. I left by the kitchen door.

Q: Did you lock the door behind you?

A: No. How could I lock it?

Q: There are locks you can just twist . . .

A: Yes, that's right, I had to . . . I tried the knob, and it wouldn't turn, so I twisted the little button on the knob, just as you say. But I didn't lock it again, I simply went out.

Q: Did you close the door behind you?

A: Yes.

Q: Did you wipe off the doorknob?

A: What?

Q: The doorknob. Did you wipe it clean?

A: No.

Q: Did you wipe off the telephone?

A: No.

Q: Or anything in the house?

A: No, I just . . . I didn't think of that. Are you talking about fingerprints?

Q: Yes.

A: I didn't think of that.

Q: What did you do when you left the house?

A: I backed the car out of the driveway, and made a wrong turn. I was very frightened, I turned in the wrong direction. Instead of the way I'd come. Through the circle there, whatever it's called. I wanted to go back to the circle. But I was heading in the opposite direction. I made a U-turn at the end of the block, and got myself straightened out. Then I drove back to the motel.

Q: What time did you get back there?

A: At a little past midnight.

Q: What did you do then?

A: I took a shower and went to sleep.

Q: What time did you wake up yesterday?
A: Around noon. I went for breakfast, and then I went back to the motel to pack. I had a reservation on the four-thirty flight.
Q: To New York?
A: Yes.
Q: You were planning to go back to New York?
A: Yes.
Q: Did you try to contact your mother again?
A: No.
Q: Or your brother?
A: No.
Q: Were you aware that he had confessed to the murders?
A: Not until later that afternoon. I didn't call him because I was afraid the police might be there on the boat questioning him, and they'd want to know who was calling him and all that. I thought . . . I still had no idea anyone had been arrested for what happened. I thought I could go back to New York and that would be the end of it.
Q: When did you learn he'd confessed?
A: On the way to the airport. I heard it on the car radio.
Q: What time was that?
A: It was on the three o'clock news.
Q: So at three o'clock yesterday, you learned that your brother had confessed to the murders?
A: Yes.
Q: What was your reaction?
A: Well, I knew he was doing it to protect me, but I didn't think he was in serious trouble because I figured he wouldn't know what to tell them.
Q: Tell who?
A: The police. If he hadn't done it, then how would he know what to tell them? I figured they'd let him go eventually. But I wasn't completely sure, so I thought I'd better *not* go back to New York just yet. Because if for some reason they started believing him . . . well, I'd just have to tell them what had really happened.
Q: Then you *didn't* go to the airport?
A: No. I went back to the motel. The woman there thought I was crazy, checking out, checking in again. I sat in

the room watching television all afternoon. At six o'clock the news came on, and the District Attorney or somebody, whatever he's called down here, said that Michael had thrown the knife in the ocean. That bothered me. I was thinking if he couldn't tell them what he'd done with the knife, why then they'd have to let him go. But if he told them he'd thrown it in the ocean . . . well, the ocean is a big place, they'd never be able to find it. They'd just have to take his word for it. So that bothered me.

Q: But still you didn't go to the police . . .

A: No. Because I wasn't sure yet. I still hoped they would let him go. I still hoped they'd think somebody else had done it, some person who just walked in off the street, you read about such people all the time. I went out to dinner at about eight, and while I was eating I decided I'd better do something about, you know, if the police ever got to me, about making sure they didn't know I'd been in Calusa since the night before. I checked out of the motel again at ten-thirty that night, there was a night clerk on by then, and I moved to the Calusa Bay Hotel. I knew the plane got in at ten, you see, and I figured if I checked in at ten-thirty, then if the police got to me, I'd just say I'd arrived in Calusa that night, and gone straight to the hotel. There'd be a record, you know, of when I checked in. This was when I still thought they'd let Michael go. I was hoping they'd let him go, but at the same time I had to protect myself. He was the only one who knew I was in Calusa, you see, I hadn't even spoken to my mother. And I knew *he* wouldn't . . . well, he was accepting the guilt for me, so I knew he wouldn't tell the police anything about me getting there earlier. On Sunday instead of Monday.

Q: When did you decide to go to the police?

A: This morning. I'd spoken to Mr. Hope last night, I'd asked him to come to the hotel so I could show him the letter I received from Michael, I thought if I could convince *him*, then maybe he'd convince the police as well. But I didn't seem able to convince him—not about Michael, not about my father either.

When I put on the news this morning, and there was nothing about the police letting Michael go, I knew then that he was in serious trouble, that they weren't going to let him go, that they were going to send him to the electric chair for something I'd done. So I got dressed and I . . . I came here.

Q: Miss Purchase, you know we have a signed confession from your brother, don't you?

A: Yes, but he was lying. He didn't kill them.

Q: How do we know *you're* not lying to protect *him?*

A: I'm not.

Q: How do we know *this* isn't a false confession, Miss Purchase?

A: Because I know where the knife is.

I had not been back to Jacaranda since the night of the murders.

Now, at a little past noon, it looked drowsy and peaceful. Many homeowners up and down the street, tired of the constant struggle against browning grass, had seeded their lawns with pebbles, giving them the serene appearance of Japanese gardens strewn with oases of cactus and palm. The sunlight was dazzling on the dappled stones. We drove up the street slowly, almost like a cortege, the car from the State's Attorney's office in the lead, the unmarked Police Department car following.

I was in the car with Bensell and Karin; she had insisted that I hear every word. She told us again how she had backed out of the driveway and turned in the wrong direction, driving *away* from where she really wanted to go. We were moving west toward the pine forest bordering the beach. She pointed out a pair of sewers ahead, one on either side of the road. She said that on Sunday night she had stopped her car, and thrown the knife in the sewer there on the right. We pulled to the curb. Car doors slammed; the street echoed with sound and then was still again. Ehrenberg and Di Luca came walking over from the second car.

"This is where she says she threw the knife," Bensell said. "Down the sewer here."

The sewer opening was little more than a narrow metal rectangle set into the cement curb. There were no sidewalks on the street; lawns of grass or pebbles stretched immediately to the roadway, where they sloped into asphalt. But the sewer had been built into a concrete mini-sidewalk some four feet square, and a cast-iron manhole cover afforded easy access to the drain below. Di Luca went back to the car for a crowbar, and then pried off the cover. In the house across the street, a woman watched from inside her screened lanai. Ehrenberg rolled the cover onto a patch of parched grass. The sewer was relatively shallow, some three or four feet deep. An inch or so of water lay stagnant on the bottom; it had not rained in Calusa all month long. Resting in the water on a bed of sand and silt was a knife with a ten-inch blade.

"Is that the knife you used to kill them?" Bensell asked.

"That's the knife," she said.

It was a little past one when we got back to the police station.

Michael was still in his cell on the second floor; I could only assume he had not yet been moved across the street because of the new developments in the case. I followed the jailer down the long corridor, watched him insert the color-coded key into the keyway. He swung the steel door back, and did not lock it behind him. We walked past the row of cells to the bend in the corridor, and then to Michael's cell. The jailer opened the barred door for me, and then locked me in. Michael was sitting on the grimy foam-rubber mattress. I heard the metal door clanging shut around the bend in the corridor, heard the key being twisted again.

I told Michael that his sister had confessed to the murders. I told him that she had led them to where she'd thrown the murder weapon down a sewer, and that Ehrenberg was fairly certain they would be able to recover latent prints and blood samples from the knife. There were cracks and crevices in the handle, and blood would have caked in it someplace. The water in the sewer was still, there was no possibility it could have completely washed away the blood; nor would water have had any effect on fingerprints.

I told him that the State's Attorney was dubious about fingerprints and blood proving Michael's sister had committed the murders. The way he saw it, this only proved she had transported the murder weapon to the sewer and disposed of it. I told Michael that Ehrenberg was hoping the latent prints they'd gathered all around the house would match up with his sister's—prints on the phone, the doorknob, the faucet handles in the bathroom, where she said she'd washed the blood from her hands. But Bensell had debated the value of the prints as evidence, saying they would only prove she'd been in the house and not that she'd murdered Maureen and the children.

I told Michael the police had confirmed his sister's telephone call to the marina, that the dockmaster there had told them he'd taken the call at eleven-thirty and had gone to the boat to get Michael. But Bensell said this only meant she'd called Michael, and not that she'd called him from the *house* during the time the coroner's report had stated the murders occurred—between ten and midnight. Bensell maintained that Karin could have called her brother from anywhere in Calusa, asking him to meet her at the house, where *together* they could have committed the murders. I explained that they were at this moment booking his sister for Murder One, but that they would not release *him* till they were convinced he'd had nothing to do with the commission of the crime.

"Michael," I said, "I'd like you to take a polygraph test.

"What for?"

"Because there's no way you can help your sister now. The only person you can help is yourself."

"You just told me the fingerprints wouldn't prove—"

"Michael, they'll let you go the minute they're sure you had nothing to do with this."

"I had *everything* to do with it. I killed them."

"Jesus, you're a pain in the ass!"

"Why couldn't she have stayed out of this?" he said.
"I guess for the same reason you couldn't," I said.
He looked at me. He nodded. He sighed heavily.

It was Ehrenberg's opinion, and mine as well, that Michael had blended what he *knew* had happened with what he *imagined* had happened, using his intimate knowledge of the house—and what he had found there on his arrival—to construct a scenario within a plausible setting. There had always been a problem about his motive, but if we were to accept the existence of the knife rack, for example, then why not accept his statement that he'd seized a knife from that rack? If we were to believe—that he'd kissed his dead stepmother on the mouth—and we both *did* believe it—then why not also believe he had stabbed her first? There had been no way of sorting the lies from the truth; in Michael's various tellings, all had sounded equally genuine; even the hesitations, the groping for words seemed not really a lapse in inventiveness but only the customary disorientation of a person confessing to a brutal crime.

The polygraph would accept no lies.

A trained examiner would ask Michael questions, and the machine would accurately record any changes in his blood pressure, respiration, pulse and electrodermal response. Ehrenberg was hopeful that the boy would be released before sundown, provided the test results showed what he thought they would. Bensell seemed a bit more dubious, and insisted he would not let Michael out on the street till he was absolutely certain of his innocence. They both advised me to go home. The test would take some time, and there was no sense in my hanging around. Ehrenberg promised he would call me as soon as he had the results.

I left the Public Safety Building at two-thirty that afternoon.

I didn't know where to go.

I got into the Ghia, and started driving toward the office, and then turned in the opposite direction and headed for the bay. I wanted to go home, I guess, but I didn't know where home was.

Aggie once asked me—this was last October, our love with still new then—whether we wouldn't grow tired of each other soon enough, seek new partners again, look again for the danger or the thrill or the romance or whatever it had been that caused us to discover each other in the first place. She had been sitting on the edge of the bed naked, looking out toward the marsh on the eastern side of the house; the sun had already moved over to the beach side, this was two or thereabouts in the afternoon. She said she thought the reason people enjoyed stories about love affairs was not because they secretly longed for such affairs themselves. On the contrary, most of the stories ended in affirmation of the marital bond—the sinners going back to their respective spouses at the end. She went on to speculate that the happy ending was essential to any story of marital infidelity, and then she said—

She said that maybe those two strangers meeting on a train weren't strangers at all. Maybe the woman was only Mrs. Smith as a young girl, and the man was Mr. Smith as he'd been when she first met him. The entire so-called "affair" was just a tale of their courtship and romance, a memory of more passionate times, with the "going back" at the end, the "happy ending" being a symbolic return to the humdrum safer reality of marriage. She was pleased with her idea. She waited for my approval, grinning, and then she kissed me. And then we made love again and in a little while I left her.

I drove over the causeway bridge now, and around Lucy's Circle, and then across the new bridge to Sabal. But instead of continuing on toward Stone Crab Key, I made an abrupt left turn onto Jamie's street and found myself driving slowly past the scene of the crime. The jacaranda stood leafless and flowerless in the center of the lawn. A month from now, it would explode against the sky in a glorious puff of feathery purple flowers, but now there were only naked branches and not a hint of promised bloom. I drove up the street toward West Lane, past the sewer into which the murder weapon had been dropped.

It occurred to me that Betty Purchase would probably

never realize she was as guilty of committing those murders as was her daughter. Karin had wielded the knife, but she had also been her mother's surrogate. The day Betty affixed the label "Goldilocks" to her husband's new wife was the day she'd first planted the seed of murder. Nor would she ever understand that over the years she herself had become what she considered Maureen to be—the intruder, the other woman: Goldilocks for sure.

I made a left turn at the corner, parked the car in a clearly marked NO PARKING zone, and stepped over the chain Michael Purchase had crossed on Sunday when he'd fled that blood-drenched house. In the forest, I took off my shoes and the socks I'd been wearing since yesterday. The pine needles were soft underfoot.

I did not think I would go back to Susan.

But neither did I want to spend the rest of my life with Agatha.

Just before I reached the beach, I threw the socks into the woods.

ABOUT THE AUTHOR

ED MCBAIN is Evan Hunter, but millions know him as Ed McBain, the top cop writer in the world and author of the 87th Precinct books. Praised by *The New York Times* as "the best of today's procedural school of police stories," the series now has over 53,000,000 copies in print around the world. McBain has been writing the 87th Precinct thrillers for the past twenty years. Fans can count on the realism of police activities in the series for, as the author explains, "I had to research very carefully by riding squad cars, attending police line-ups and visiting labs." Thus, the details are authentic and have become a McBain trademark.

McBain grew up on the tough city streets of New York with one main ambition: to get out. At first he thought his ticket out would be his artistic skills, but during a two year stint in the Navy, he discovered a new talent: writing short stories. When he returned two years later, he attended Hunter College, then spent a disastrous few months teaching high school. Hunter turned that experience into a sizzling novel, later made into a film, called *Blackboard Jungle*. He's been writing steadily since that time (as Ed McBain with the 87th Precinct series) and the latest Evan Hunter novel, *The Chisholms*, was a CBS TV mini-series. He's also written *Strangers When We Meet, Last Summer* and the script for Hitchcock's celebrated horror film, *The Birds*. Evan Hunter lives with his wife, Mary Vann, and their daughter, Amanda Finley. They divide their time between Connecticut and points south.